Yuri Drewes

Grand magus of the Royal Magi Assembly. His only interest is in research related to magic and magical powers.

"Are you going to try calling on the Saint's powers now?"

"That dinner was utterly divine."

Albert Hawke

Knight commander of the Knights of the Third Order. Known as the "Ice Knight" for his supposedly frigid demeanor, but toward Sei, he's...?

Leonhardt

The leader of the mercenary company in Klausner's Domain. He takes a liking to Sei for her great skill as an alchemist.

"Hmm? Are you one of Granny's apprentices?"

Sei

An office lady in her twenties who has finally been recognized as the Saint. Likes to cook and make cosmetics in her spare time.

"I happened to hear that place is sometimes referred to as the alchemist's holy land."

The Saint's Magic Power is Omnipotent

"The name's Leonhardt. I'm in charge of this castle's mercenary company."

He grinned and clapped me on the shoulder. "Pleased to meet ya."

I couldn't help but stagger.

I really wish he would learn a little restraint.

Table of Contents

The Saint's Magic Power is Omnipotent

NOVEL

3

WRITTEN BY
Yuka Tachibana

ILLUSTRATED BY
Yasuyuki Syuri

Airship

Seven Seas Entertainment

The moment she got home from working overtime at the office, Sei Takanashi, an office lady in her twenties, was abruptly summoned to another world. Although Sei was summoned to be the Saint, the crown prince of the kingdom exited the room with only Aira Misono, the cute high school girl who had been summoned with Sei, leaving Sei behind.

Sei had no notion of how to return to Japan, so she soon decided to begin working at the palace's Research Institute of Medicinal Flora.

Although Sei realized that she was indeed the Saint, she concealed the truth in order to live her life as an ordinary person. However, Sei displayed tremendous magical ability, astounding everyone with her skills in potion-making, cooking, and concocting cosmetics.

Starting from the day she used one of her high-grade HP potions to save Knight Commander Albert Hawke's life, Sei performed one miracle after another. In time, rumor in the palace began to suggest that Sei Takanashi was the true Saint.

Although she was summoned by the Royal Magi Assembly to be the Saint, Sei managed to avoid being outed for some time. She took up intensive magical training under the guidance of Grand Magus Yuri Drewes, and her days were busy yet fulfilling.

Perhaps as a result of her training, or perhaps by mere coincidence, Sei performed another miracle with her gold-colored magic, strengthening suspicions that she was the Saint. However, Crown Prince Kyle denounced those suspicions, stubbornly upholding Aira as the true Saint.

However, on a monster-slaying expedition, Sei once and for all proved her Sainthood. When Knight Commander Albert Hawke was in danger, Sei called on her golden magic to instantly cleanse the black miasma producing the monsters.

As a result, Crown Prince Kyle was confined to his quarters for accusing Sei of being a false Saint. Furthermore, Aira, who had been isolated by Kyle once she arrived in the kingdom, was finally able to make friends at the academy, and with Sei. She, too, now strives for a peaceful life.

THE SAINT'S MAGIC POWER IS OMNIPOTENT VOL. 3

© Yuka Tachibana, Yasuyuki Syuri 2018
Illustrated by Yasuyuki Syuri

First published in Japan in 2018 by
KADOKAWA CORPORATION, Tokyo.
English translation rights arranged with
KADOKAWA CORPORATION, Tokyo.

Seven Seas press and purchase enquiries can be sent to
Marketing Manager Lianne Sentar at press@gomanga.com.
Information regarding the distribution and purchase of
digital editions is available from Digital Manager CK Russell
at digital@gomanga.com.

Follow Seven Seas Entertainment online at
sevenseasentertainment.com.

TRANSLATION: Julie Goniwich
COVER DESIGN: Nicky Lim
LOGO DESIGN: George Panella
INTERIOR LAYOUT & DESIGN: Clay Gardner
PROOFREADER: Jade Gardner, Rebecca Schneidereit
LIGHT NOVEL EDITOR: E.M. Candon
PREPRESS TECHNICIAN: Rhiannon Rasmussen-Silverstein
PRODUCTION MANAGER: Lissa Pattillo
MANAGING EDITOR: Julie Davis
ASSOCIATE PUBLISHER: Adam Arnold
PUBLISHER: Jason DeAngelis

ISBN: 978-1-64827-205-9
Printed in Canada
First Printing: May 2021
10 9 8 7 6 5 4 3 2 1

IT HAD BEEN A YEAR since my summoning. The seasons had cycled, and spring was on the horizon. However, we were as yet mired in the end of winter. Although milder than in Japan, the climate near the capital city was still cold.

Despite the chill, I had taken myself yet again to the Royal Magi Assembly's practice grounds to train with my magic.

The grounds were outside, but I wore only a light robe on top of my regular clothes—rather than, you know, a proper coat. I could get away with such lightweight clothing because the robe was enchanted with Fire Magic. It formed a layer of warm air around my body when worn, like a personal heater, and it made being outdoors in this weather quite comfortable.

Grand Magus Yuri Drewes had gifted me this convenient—and expensive—item. He'd claimed he was giving it to me because he didn't want me to catch a cold, but I suspected his generosity came only half from kindness. The other half likely stemmed from some kind of ulterior motive.

Just as I was casting a Holy Magic spell as a warm-up exercise, Yuri arrived at the practice grounds. *Speak of the devil and all that.*

"You have improved considerably." Wearing a painted-on smile on his handsome face, he looked beautiful as ever. However, looks can be deceiving.

This may sound rude, but in truth, Yuri was well known to be single-mindedly obsessed with magic. It was quite a shame, really.

"Thank you," I said.

Yuri dispensed with the pleasantries and jumped immediately to what he wanted to know. "Are you going to try calling on the Saint's powers now?"

"Yes. I just finished warming up."

By "the Saint's powers," he was referring to the magic I had used in the western forest, which had dissipated the miasma swamp and all the monsters it belched up in one fell swoop.

Despite his numerous obligations, Yuri always came

to join me during my daily post-lesson practice, but only because he wanted to see me use the Saint's magic again. I was pretty sure that had something to do with why he'd given me the enchanted robe as well.

I could see the glimmer in his eye as he waited for me to cast again. I felt bad keeping him waiting, so I prepared myself.

I looked away from Yuri, took a deep breath, and summoned my conviction. Why did I have to do all this? Because since our return from the western forest, I hadn't managed to cast the spell again.

The research institute and the western forest—these were the only two places I had managed to use the Saint's magic, but I still had no idea exactly *how* I had done it.

I had been told that I must have tapped into my powers as the Saint both times, but, well, each time, the effects of the magic had been different. The first time, I had improved the effectiveness of herbs. The second, I eliminated the black swamp that we suspected had been created by the miasma.

However, one thing had been the same each time: the gold color of the magic. When this golden magic suddenly burst forth from inside me, it always felt as though it was literally pouring out of me. Therefore, since I remembered how it *felt* when I cast the magic, I had a feeling that if I could just figure out how to summon up that feeling, the rest would be easy.

The problem was that I had no clue where to start. I had tried a ton of different things, but I still hadn't figured it out. This feeling of groping around in the dark searching for an answer gave me traumatic flashbacks to working in Japan.

Stop that, self. I gotta concentrate on the magic now. I refocused myself on the magical power circulating through my body. Thanks to months of training, I could now identify the feel of the magic in my body the moment I focused. I examined that magic, but I didn't find any sign of the golden kind I was hoping for.

But if I recall correctly, at the time, there was some kind of bursting feeling in my chest. Hmm. Hmm, hmm, hmm...

A few minutes later, I dropped my concentration and let out a sigh. How in the world was I supposed to figure out how this magic worked? I didn't remember doing anything special at either time, let alone anything specifically magical.

"Is it difficult?" Yuri asked.

"Yeah, I still have no idea how to put my finger on it."

"I apologize for not watching your process more closely back in the forest."

"Really, it's not something you should be apologizing about."

"But I really, truly regret that I was unable to verify how it worked. If only I had properly observed the magic, then by now, we could be..." he sighed.

Let me put it this way: At the time when I cast the magic, everyone was busy trying to stay alive, including Yuri. Nevertheless, when we got back to the palace, he had been devastated by my inability to call on the powers of the Saint again. If I *had* figured out how to use the Saint's magic on command, right about now I would probably be subject to Yuri's various experiments.

In short, the rest of Yuri's sentence was probably supposed to be something like "by now, we could be in the thick of so, so, so many different trials."

And thus, I spent the rest of the day trying my hardest to use the magic again, only to come up with nothing.

One cold day in spring, I had stayed cooped up in the institute all day since I didn't feel like going outside.

"Sei, are you making *more* potions?" Jude asked.

"Yup, that's right. We've been getting a lot more orders lately, you see." I'd had this conversation a number of times since coming to this world.

"But aren't you making way more than necessary again?"

"You think so?" I tilted my head as I looked at the potions before me. I heard Jude sigh deeply.

You don't have to sound that exasperated. I wasn't lying about there being more orders.

At first, I'd only made potions for the Knights of the Third Order, but now I was making them for the Second Order and the Royal Magi Assembly as well. You see, the whole palace now knew the rumor that the potions made at the institute were more effective than those made anywhere else.

This wasn't the only reason for the order backlog, though. Due to the influx of monsters in recent years, there was a high demand for potions in the general market as well, and for a long time now, there had been a widespread shortage. A layperson might think we should therefore just increase how many potions we made, but the matter wasn't so easily resolved.

Potions couldn't be made just by following a recipe. The higher-ranking potions required subtle magical manipulation, and the maker needed to have the appropriate skill level in Pharmaceuticals. If the maker's level was lower than the rank of the potion they wanted to make, their attempt would fail, and they'd be left with a bunch of boiled plant matter.

As a result, while there were quite a few people who could make mid-grade potions, very few could reliably produce high-grade ones. Also, since potion-making required magic, the number of potions a person could make in a day was limited by the amount of MP they possessed. Once they ran out, they were unable to make any more until they rested or drank an MP potion. This limitation was considered the main reason why raising one's Pharmaceuticals skill was so difficult.

Therefore, the problem couldn't be solved simply by "making more potions"—the world was already producing them at capacity.

Potions were a particular necessity for the knightly Orders, due to their value during monster-slaying expeditions. With the increase in the monster population around the capital, the number of required potions had also soared.

However, even though the palace got first dibs on newly produced potion batches, they couldn't monopolize the market. While high-grade potions were expensive and out of reach for most commoners, low-grade ones were largely obtainable. If the palace bought those up too, they would foster discontent among the common folk.

The palace officials recognized this and as a result closely managed the palace's potion consumption. Thus, although they had increased the amount of potions they procured for the knightly Orders, they were unable to acquire any more than they already did. As such, the knights were forced to let minor injuries heal on their own, while mages who could use Holy Magic were asked to tend the more dire wounds.

All of this was why the potions made at our institute had caught everyone's attention. Not only were they more effective, we were able to produce more per day than the medicine shops in the capital. The Orders couldn't resist jumping at them after enduring the chronic shortage of years past.

"Maybe they did put in more orders, but I doubt they increased them by *this* much," Jude said.

"I swear I'm keeping the requested number in mind while I make them."

"Really? I kind of doubt they'd ever order *this* many high-grade HP potions. Johan's gonna yell at you again."

All the potions lined up in neat rows before me were indeed the high-grade variety. The herbs required to make them were expensive, so they weren't used unless absolutely necessary. And...fine, Jude was right. The Orders hadn't ordered *quite* as many as I'd made.

But I only made so many because I wanted to raise my Pharmaceuticals skill, which I could only do by making potions. However, my level was now so high that even making high-grade potions wasn't increasing it.

Given the cost of the requisite ingredients, Johan had told me to stop making so many of them...and I was *trying* to be careful about my quota, I really was, but... *Oof, I guess I wound up making too many after all.*

"What about the other kinds the Orders asked for? Don't you have to make those?" Jude asked.

"Oh, I did."

"What? You're done already?"

"The majority of what they asked for were low- and mid-grade potions, you know."

Jude had told me before that I could make far more potions in a day than the average professional alchemist. So many more, in fact, that it would take most alchemists multiple days to match what I could cough up in just one.

I suspected this had something to do with my absurdly high base level. An individual's base level determined their maximum HP and MP, and from what I had heard, alchemists typically weren't even at Level 10. Logically, since making potions required imbuing a brew with magical power, people who had more MP could make more potions. I didn't know exactly how *much* more MP I had than someone at Level 10, but I was pretty sure the difference was, shall we say, considerable.

As Jude and I were talking, Johan appeared.

Speak of the other devil! I thought.

"Sei, there you are, there's something I need to—" Johan's gaze froze on the high-grade HP potions on my desk.

Eep. It was just like him to pop up before I could put them away!

"Hm. I don't mind your professional enthusiasm, but I think you've overdone it a bit," he said.

"Sorry..."

I really had been keeping the specific request in mind when making them. However, the amount of vials on my desk exceeded the request by an order of two, maybe even three.

Johan must have realized that, but he didn't scold me. Given the sheer amount of overkill, I would have grimly accepted any admonishment, which was why I apologized when I saw him looking at me with that familiar exasperation.

"Well, as it turns out, I wanted to talk to you about potions," he said.

"You...you did?"

The unusual seriousness of his expression made me tremble with fear. Was this the day he cracked? Was I in for the reprimand of a lifetime? I straightened my posture and made myself look attentive as Johan began.

"You're not going to be making any more potions for the time being."

"Huh?! Why not?"

"Because it's become difficult to acquire the ingredients."

"What?!"

Johan went on to explain that fewer herbs than usual had been imported to the capital this past fall. The harvest from the domain where most herbs came from had been frightfully small this year, so there was a shortage of herbs in markets everywhere.

The shops we procured our supplies from had been working hard to make sure the institute got its usual deliveries, but it had finally started to become difficult for them to source our orders. Johan had just received word that, for the time being, none of our orders could be filled.

"Well, that sounds bad," I said.

"Yes. I had heard back in the fall that there might be a shortage, but I hadn't imagined they would outright halt deliveries."

"How long do you think it will be before we can order again?"

"We can't say for sure, but the shopkeepers think it's likely to take a while."

"That's *really* bad."

The domain in question exported not only the herbs that went into low-grade potions but those required for mid- and high-grade potions as well. Normally, the ingredients for low-grade potions were relatively easy to cultivate regardless of local climate. However, the herbs for mid-grade potions were a bit more difficult to grow. They didn't take in regular soil, and it required some effort to nurture them. The ones in the institute's gardens depended entirely on the hard work of our researchers.

In the domain that supplied herbs, there were a few tracts of land where mid-grade potion ingredients grew with little to no effort, so they were vigorously cultivated as a prime local product. This same area also had a forest where the herbs used in high-grade potions grew wild, so they exported those as well.

After a meticulous harvest, these herbs were transported to the capital. However, sometimes the universe interfered and the period during which they could be transported deviated from expectations, which was what Johan believed had caused the scarcity in the fall. Though supply had increased since that early shortage, it hadn't yet recovered, and now we faced a total stoppage.

Johan wasn't the only one who believed that there had to be some kind of problem at the site of origin—the officials in the palace did as well. Therefore, they were sending an investigative team from the palace to the domain.

"What will we do about the orders from the knights?" I asked.

"The only thing we can do right now is stop filling them."

"Mm, understood."

Having said what he needed to, Johan returned to his office. Jude and I went back to our own work as well. However, since I had been told to stop making potions, I didn't exactly have more work to do.

I couldn't help thinking as I cleaned up my work station. There weren't as many monsters around the capital now, but the knights were still going out on their expeditions... But now they wouldn't have as many potions, even though they were still going to need them. If this shortage continued, sooner or later something bad was bound to happen.

I sure hope things go back to normal soon.

One early afternoon after class, I was quietly flipping through a book in a corner of the palace library. I'd had magic class that day, so it would have been a better use of my time to head over to the practice grounds, but I just wasn't in the mood, so I was poking around in the library instead.

I had picked out an herbology encyclopedia. It contained detailed drawings of herbs and descriptions of their benefits. I had read this book once before, but I was zeroing in on some new interesting tidbits this time.

As I picked it over at length, something suddenly occurred to me: the book listed all the parts of the country where herbs were grown, and a certain name kept popping up. I nonchalantly flipped back in the book and found that numerous herbs came from that same place, including the ones used in both HP and MP potions, as well as those used in potions for curing status abnormalities.

They must export a ton, I thought, and then I remembered where I had heard of this place before—it was the very domain that had recently stopped shipping as many herbs.

It sounded like it really was an herb-picker's paradise, just like you'd expect from somewhere known for its premium exports. I had no idea what was causing its recent shipping troubles, but the scope of the impact had to be even huger than I'd imagined, considering how many herbs seemed to be sourced from there. Even ordinary citizens used potions to cure status abnormalities from time to time, after all.

Maybe it was just my personality to fixate on a thing once it occurred to me, but I was starting to consider investing some serious time in learning more about this region.

Just then, I heard the library door open with a creak, and I spotted a head of fluffy brown hair enter through it.

"Oh, Sei!"

"Oh, hi there," I greeted the girl.

She was Aira Misono, the other girl who had been summoned to this world at the same time as me. In about a month, she was going to graduate from the academy she was attending. *I wonder what she's doing here at the library.*

"Don't you have class right now?" I asked.

"Not today. I was actually just on my way to the Magi Assembly, but there was something I wanted to look into first."

Aira told me that classes were already over for those who were going to graduate this year, so she only had to go to school if she wanted, while those with bad grades were busy taking supplementary classes. It didn't sound all that different from high school in Japan.

Aira received excellent grades, and moreover she had decided to join the Royal Magi Assembly upon graduation. Therefore, she had decided it would be more worth her time to go to the Assembly to do self-study instead of take supplementary classes at the academy.

She was proficient in not only Holy Magic, but Water and Wind as well. However, until recently, she had been solely focused on raising her Holy Magic level, so with her new ambition, she had been training more in the other elements. Her skills were increasing at a remarkable rate. In fact, since so few people were proficient in multiple elements, the mages were hopeful that Aira would become one of their top-ranking mages once she leveled up.

She was currently taking the same kind of classes and training that I was, but there was a theory she was having trouble understanding, so she had dropped by the library to try to figure it out.

While the Royal Magi Assembly had a ton of literature regarding magic, most of it was extremely technical and difficult for a beginner to understand. I had come to the library to learn more about magic myself in the past, so I knew how Aira felt.

"Are you here for research as well?" Aira asked.

"Yup, herbs again. Oh, but, if possible, please keep the fact that I'm here a secret."

"Ah, okay." Aira smiled wryly.

Why did I want my presence to be a secret? Surely it wasn't hard to guess.

Lately, a full third of all my magic classes had been dedicated to one topic: the Saint's powers. I was still having trouble summoning them and was no closer to understanding how to do so.

That might have been a more bearable problem if it weren't for the fact that Yuri was still upset that he wasn't able to research my Saintly powers to his heart's content. He had continued to accompany me to the practice grounds after lessons, but his patience was clearly reaching its limit. He was now using my class time to try and trigger my magic.

If Lord Smarty-Glasses hadn't stepped in, the whole class probably would have descended into Yuri's Research Bonanza. It was thanks to Erhart's interference that I was only losing a third of my study time to Yuri's insatiable curiosity.

As such, I asked Aira to keep my location a secret because I didn't want Yuri to know where I was hiding. If he found out I was reading a book about herbs instead of on the practice grounds, he would surely come swooping in to drag me off for more prodding. No doubt about it. Even the other mages would agree with that assessment.

And sure, I was interested in my powers as the Saint. I could use them to enhance herbs, for one. However, it was taking a bit of a mental toll to devote so much time to something I just couldn't do. That was probably part of why I didn't feel like heading to the practice grounds in the first place.

"I had thought medicinal herbs were unique to this world, but it seems like they aren't," Aira said with a hint of nostalgia as she peered at the book I was reading. The page I had opened to just happened to feature an herb that was common back in Japan, too.

"That's right," I said. "Back home we called them just herbs, but they consider them to be *medicinal* herbs here."

After a bit more conversation, I heard the library door open again. We both looked up to find Liz had entered.

"A good day to you both," she said.

"Heya. Long time no see," I said.

"Hello," said Aira.

It felt like it had been ages since I last saw Liz in the library. Despite all the tension between her and the crown prince, Liz was still being educated at the palace to become the future queen. Unlike Aira and the prince, she still had one more year before she graduated from the academy. As a result, it was no exaggeration to say that her days were mostly spent traveling between the academy and the palace. She was a terribly busy young woman.

I had been pretty busy myself since I started taking classes. Our constant missing each other was, in that light, inevitable.

"I see you are reading up on medicinal herbs again." Liz peered at my book and smiled.

You know, it was likely that every time we saw each other here, I had a different herbology book open.

"It's been a nice change of pace," I told her.

"Even though it's work-related?"

"Finding different uses for the essential oils you can extract from plants has been an interest of mine for a long time."

"Do you mean like for aromatherapy?" Aira asked.

"Exactly."

"What's 'aroma therapy'?" Liz asked with a quizzical look.

"Well, it's..."

Aira and I began to explain the concept to her. As we talked, the topic gradually shifted to the recent herb shortage.

"We have been talking for quite a while. Are we keeping you longer than we should, Sei?" Liz asked.

"Nah, I'm fine—this reading counts as the research part of my job. Plus, it's not like I can make potions even if I do go back to the institute."

"Whyever not?"

"Well, you know, because of the shortage. We no longer have ingredients, so my boss put a moratorium on all potion creation."

"Now that you mention it, I do recall hearing such a thing. The prices of herbs have gone up everywhere."

"Have you ever heard of Klausner's Domain? Apparently it's famous for its herb varieties."

"Indeed I have. It's sometimes called the alchemist's holy land."

"Is that so?"

Klausner was the name of the lord who ruled over the region where the herb shortage had started. All the regions in the Kingdom of Salutania were referred to using the name of their respective feudal lord. I wanted Liz's opinion on the topic, seeing as she was receiving education fit for a queen, which included knowing all the ins and outs of the regions in the kingdom.

I gave her a quizzical look at the mention of a "holy land," and this time it was Liz and Aira who explained something to me.

(Aira knew about Klausner's Domain thanks to her

classes at the academy. Maybe she was taking a geography class?)

In any case, according to them, Klausner's Domain was known not only for its high yield and wide variety in medicinal herbs but for the potions they developed in the region.

It was also said that herbs grew in such abundance and variety that the locals had developed unique potions that weren't well recorded. In fact, every family of alchemists in Klausner's Domain had secret recipes for potions that had been handed down through generations. For ages, countless alchemists had visited the domain in order to learn how to make these secret potions, which was why the region had come to be called the alchemist's holy land.

"Wow, so they make a real diverse spread, huh?" I said.

"That's correct," said Liz. "I have never been, but my father has."

"Did he see the actual potions?"

"Yes, and he has even seen them being used. One of their test subjects was someone who worked for my family, and he reported that the effects of the potion weren't the least bit exaggerated, either."

"Really, now?" I was starting to feel kind of excited hearing about all these secret recipes and so forth. Perhaps one of them might even exceed the strength of your typical high-grade HP potion? *I wonder if I could convince them to teach me how to make it!*

After we all went our separate ways, I was still distracted with all sorts of thoughts about these unknown potions.

"Huh?"

As I walked down a hall in the institute, carrying a box of potions, I happened to glance out a window and spot Knight Commander Albert's horse entering our courtyard. *Well, that's odd. Does he need to talk to Johan?*

Usually, it was Johan who went to the knights' barracks when he and Albert needed to consult with each other. Albert only came to the institute when he was escorting me home.

By the time I reached the entrance, Albert was just coming in. "Sei, always a pleasure. Is Johan in?"

"Yup. He's in his office."

"Thanks."

He immediately set off in the correct direction. I didn't even have to tell him where it was.

Hoo boy. This looks like it might take a while. And he came all this way on horseback—I bet he could use some refreshments. I put my box of potions by my station and headed to the dining hall to make some tea.

Once I had a nice little platter, I made my way to Johan's office and knocked before entering. "Pardon me."

Johan and Albert looked up as I joined them, their expressions somewhat grim. Whatever they were talking about, Albert's sudden arrival meant it required immediate attention. I had no doubt it was troubling news at best.

However, since this was a conversation between the head researcher of the Research Institute of Medicinal Flora and the knight commander of the Knights of the Third Order, it was above my pay grade, so to speak. I intended to leave the tea and cookies and go. But when I tried to make my exit, Johan stopped me.

"Would you like to join us?" Johan had recovered his usual smile as he asked.

"Aren't you two talking about something important?"

"We're finished."

Is this really okay? It seemed so urgent. And I'm kind of on the clock myself. Also, if we're having tea, I'd rather like to get a cup, too... Oh, fine, why not?

I admit—even if whatever was going on was none of my business, I was a little worried. How could I not be after seeing those grim faces? Especially considering how important these guys were!

I sat down next to Johan and glanced at Albert just as he was taking a sip of his tea. I watched his Adam's apple bob as he swallowed, and the wrinkle on his brow faded away. After taking a bite of a cookie, his expression calmed, too.

That initially gave me a bit of relief, but then Albert met my eye.

Ack, I'm staring at him again!

Even worse, Albert had the nerve to smile in that intimate, inviting way of his, and it just made me so incandescently self-conscious that I had to avert my gaze.

"Hey, have you two forgotten I'm here?" Johan said irritably.

"Of course we haven't!" I protested, but I don't think I sounded all that convincing—even though it was the truth. How could I forget my boss was in the room?

"Al's going to be leaving the capital for a bit," Johan said suddenly with a sidelong glance at me.

"Huh?"

I looked to Albert and found him wearing an uneasy smile. "As you know, the situation around the capital isn't nearly as dire as it was. Therefore, it's been decided that I'll be heading out to the countryside next."

"You mean because the miasma's gone—as well as the monsters?"

"Yes."

"Is everyone from the Third Order going?"

"Not everyone, but the majority will be coming with me."

Only one thought entered my mind, and it hung there, inescapable: *It's finally happening.*

Now that spring was nearly here, it would be easier to travel than it had been during the winter. It was the ideal season for long trips. But that wasn't what had made this turn of events inevitable.

Despite that inevitability, I still felt tense—perhaps from anxiety. Or maybe I had let myself relax and fantasize about futures that could never be, seeing as it had been a few months since our excursion to the western forest.

Immediately after our return, there had been rumors that the number of monsters near the capital had drastically decreased. The knightly Orders had continued to conduct monster-slaying expeditions, and they had also reported a reduction in monster population, but the higher-ups hadn't wanted to make assumptions, and so we'd been in a bit of a holding pattern.

But now months had passed, and it seemed they had confirmed for themselves that the monsters weren't likely to return. As a result, the palace had grown more confident that the capital was finally safe.

At the same time, a flood of requests had come pouring in from the countryside nobility—requests for the knightly Orders to be dispatched to their domains.

Unlike in the capital, the number of monsters in the countryside continued to increase, and the situation was growing desperate.

It wasn't like these nobles weren't doing anything. They all employed mercenary companies to fend off monsters in their respective domains, and despite the recent spike in the monster population, they had managed to deal with the threat by sending out more frequent expeditions of their own. However, there was a limit to how much any mercenary, company, or noble could do.

In times past, the palace had dispatched the knightly Orders to provide additional aid whenever a given noble lacked the personnel to deal with threats to their people. Now that word of the capital's newfound peace had spread, those nobles were all hoping the palace would send their knights, just like they once had.

"Where are you headed?" I asked Albert tentatively.

"Klausner's Domain, for the time being. We'll also be checking in on other domains along the way."

"Oh—the domain that exports all those herbs?"

"That's right."

Huh. That name just kept popping up again and again. In any case, this certainly explained some things.

"The palace must be troubled by the herb shortage," said Johan—which was exactly what I was thinking.

"Indeed. It's been a problem for your institute, too, hasn't it, Johan?" Albert asked.

"Yes, and I'm sure it's impacting the knights as well."

"You're not wrong. Although we're not facing as many monsters now, we still have to go out and exterminate the rest."

And whenever they did that, injuries were a given. They needed potions. We all did. No wonder the palace had decided it was so critical to finally dispatch their knights.

"When are you guys going to leave?" I asked.

"We have to make some preparations, but I think in about two weeks."

"Two weeks? Okay." I nodded. "I'll get myself prepared, too."

"Get yourself prepared?" Albert asked. He and Johan eyed me with suspicion.

Huh?

"What do you need to prepare for? Oh wait, do you mean preparing potions for the expeditions?" asked Johan.

"Yeah, of course, but I need to get lots of other things ready, too, right? Like clothes, and—"

"Whose clothes?"

Their expressions remained unchanged. I got the feeling we were all on different wavelengths. Had I jumped to the wrong conclusion?

"Wait, don't tell me you're planning on going, too?" Johan asked as if having some kind of epiphany.

"Uh, yeah? Hadn't we talked about that?"

From the way they were looking at me with such surprise, it seemed my going anywhere hadn't been on the table until now.

That's odd. Didn't we have a whole discussion about this just a couple months ago?

"I guess it might have come up..." Johan trailed off.

"Would it be better if I stayed behind this time, considering my current...situation? I mean, I wouldn't say I'd be *completely* useless—since I can use Holy Magic and all." I made my inquiry cautiously, shrinking down a little.

By "current situation," I was referring to the little problem with me not being able to call up the Saint's power whenever I wanted. Johan seemed to catch my drift, his look serious. That was fair. What help could I be to an expedition if I couldn't cast that critical magic?

However, my Holy Magic would still be useful in a support role, what with all the healing spells I could cast. Although it wasn't like I was the only person who could do that—other people had Holy Magic too, even if no one was at my level. That in itself wasn't an argument in favor of my necessity.

Johan's eyes got a far-off, calculating look to them. "You seem pretty excited about this."

"Uh..."

"You're hiding something, aren't you? Out with it."

Okay, okay. Until now, I had avoided any topic that had to do with being the Saint like the plague, so of course my sudden enthusiasm made him wary. In fact, way back when, I had been very much the opposite of enthusiastic about the prospect of joining future countryside expeditions. Perhaps obviously, I'd much rather have spent my time doing research at the institute.

But, well... "I, uh, happened to hear that Klausner's Domain is sometimes referred to as the alchemist's holy land."

And with that, Johan's expression turned from suspicion to exasperation.

I'm sorry! I just have a feeling I'd never get to go if it weren't for this opportunity.

Albert looked confused, seemingly still catching up to

the gist of our conversation. Johan sighed and explained a bit of what was meant by that nickname, and as he did, Albert's lips quirked into a grin.

"Well, so that's how it is," he said. "You want to expand your knowledge there, right, Sei?"

"I do." I reflexively dropped my gaze, feeling awkward, not to mention a bit worried that my reasoning was actually pretty frivolous—I mean, Albert and his knights were going to be risking their lives.

However, neither Albert nor Johan seemed bothered in the least.

"Well, to tell you the truth, there's a veritable treasure trove of herbology knowledge in Klausner's Domain—things we don't have record of here in the capital. It might actually be a good thing for you to go there and learn from an alchemist or two," Johan said.

"The knights would be stationed there for some time, too," Albert added.

"Does that mean I can go?" I looked at them each in turn, which earned me some oddly tight smiles from both.

"Actually, I'd like to ask you to," Johan said.

"In fact, the palace has already requested your presence," Albert added.

"They did?"

"I'm afraid so. However, we were initially opposed... and were just discussing how best to turn them down."

They explained their reticence was based in the as yet finicky nature of my Saintly power. They were worried that if I wasn't able to cast the magic again, I would be subject to criticism from not only the palace but the people of Salutania. My general lack of interest in monster slaying was another reason for their opposition.

"Ah. I apologize for causing so much distress," I said.

"No, please don't worry. We were the ones who pushed you."

"That's right. Don't trouble yourself with it."

The two of them smiled as they insisted I shouldn't worry. I felt kind of bad, since I was suddenly sure they had been having meetings like this for a while—especially as, now that I thought about it, I hadn't really experienced any unpleasantness from the palace since I started living at the institute.

"Thank you for all you've done for me," I added with a short bow.

"Hmm? Why do you say that?"

"No particular reason..."

Both of them looked at me curiously.

Perhaps to them this consideration for my feelings was only natural and not worth being thanked for, but I was grateful to them anyway. However, I felt too shy to explain any of that, so I just shrugged off their peering with a smile as I thanked them yet again in my thoughts.

The Saint's
Magic Power is
Omnipotent

Behind the Scenes I

"AND THAT CONCLUDES my report."

"Thank you."

The king of Salutania watched the official who had just given his report leave and waited until his office door closed before he heaved a sigh. The prime minister, who was with him, also wore a dark expression. The atmosphere in the room weighed on them both.

The king picked up one of the documents on his desk. "There's been no change in the countryside?"

"Correct. Rather, with the situation in the capital settling down, the number of petitions continues to increase."

"I see."

Following Sei's annihilation of the black swamp that had appeared in the western forest, there had been a significant decrease in the local monster population. In fact, their numbers had returned to what was considered tolerably normal.

Thus far, wanting to be cautious with Sei's safety, the king and his prime minister had done their best to keep circumspect about the Saint. But the relative absence of monsters near the capital was too significant a change to deny.

The nobles had already talked amongst themselves about the successful summoning of the Saint from another world, and now they would inevitably whisper of her most recent deeds.

Even the nobles who had previously kept silent were beginning to act. These lords, who presided over the countryside, had shown understanding for the palace's inability to send knights to help them. However, with the capital now stabilized, their appeals for aid were growing more frequent and fervent, claiming they were nearing their limits and begging for assistance.

The king and other officials understood the dangers of the situation, and they were indeed planning to call on the knights in short order. That wasn't the issue. The problem was the Saint.

Some of the lords had taken to loudly insisting that their domain was in greater peril than any other, and these lords also demanded that the palace send the Saint herself to their territory.

"I know we predicted this would happen, but we simply can't answer every one of these requests," the king said.

"Assuming that we consider dispatching the Saint at a later date, when it's safe, all we can do for now is prioritize sending the knights to each domain in turn based on the gravity of the situation."

"You speak truth. In which case, Klausner's has the greatest need, wouldn't you say?"

A pile of petitions from every territory sat upon the king's desk. Every petition had been exhaustively investigated by bureaucrats before making its way there, and all these were from domains that likely possessed a black swamp similar to the one encountered in the western forest.

At the top of the stack loomed the petition from Klausner's Domain, known for its medicinal herbs. Its crisis had been determined to be most dire, hence its place on the top.

The king looked over the document in one hand with the other on his chin. "The monsters certainly are a problem there, but the bigger problem is the trouble they're having with cultivation."

"Is that why there was a decrease in shipments to the capital?"

"It appears so."

The king handed the document over to the prime minister, who sighed heavily upon reading it.

The petition from Klausner's Domain reported that the increase in monsters was impacting their harvest. The company of mercenaries Klausner employed was no longer able to keep them at bay.

If Klausner's Domain had been anything other than the lead exporter of medicinal herbs, it likely wouldn't have been labeled a priority. However, due to this status, their troubles meant a key military resource was under threat, especially as some of the herbs they cultivated couldn't be sourced elsewhere.

It went without saying that the Lord Klausner himself was well aware of his domain's precious resources. While he wasn't alone in employing a mercenary company, his company was far stronger than those found elsewhere. The maintenance of such an excellent company required significant funds, and it was well known that Lord Klausner paid that handsome sum himself in order to avoid depending on the palace.

The fact that Lord Klausner was demanding knightly support despite his capable mercenaries meant the situation was grim indeed. It went without saying that the officials were uniformly alarmed.

"This is troubling, to say the least. Do we expect to see impact in the market?" the king asked.

"We temporarily halted deliveries to the palace, and I ordered some staff to secure stock for the market, but I fear it's likely we already have."

According to Klausner's petition, the harvest was half what it had been the previous year. Recent years had seen a gradual decline in the harvest, but this sudden drop was decidedly abnormal.

As the lord of a land whose main export was herbs, Lord Klausner likely felt an intense sense of impending crisis. No wonder that had spurred his decision to send the petition.

The king rested his elbows on his desk and folded his hands together. He dropped his gaze, mulling the situation over for a moment before finally murmuring, "Because of the monsters..."

He was thinking of the swamp they had discovered in the western forest—the swamp Sei had eliminated with her mysterious powers, which they suspected had been created from miasma.

Two facts undergirded this hypothesis. The first was that monsters had emerged from the swamp, and it was known that monsters were borne from a certain density of miasma. Knight Commander Hawke of the Third

Order and his knights, who had accompanied Sei on this expedition, had furthermore reported that the miasma grew denser the closer they drew to the swamp.

The second reason was that while they had no way to tell how long the swamp had been in the forest, the clear decrease in the monster population coincided with its elimination. Scouts sent to monitor the area where the swamp had been also reported that the miasma was gradually thinning.

They referred to the phenomenon as a "swamp" because of its muddy, black appearance, but in his report, Grand Magus Yuri Drewes had suggested it might be more accurately thought of as a spring from which the miasma gushed forth.

Based on the situation described in Klausner's petition, it was possible a similar swamp had appeared in his domain. That meant there was just one real solution to this problem.

The king wasn't the only one who had come to this conclusion. Studying his king's expression, the prime minister said, "We may need to ask the Saint to go now."

The king nodded slowly. They had reached no official conclusion, but despite the fact that they had identified a solution for their problem, the king and prime minister were weighed down by the same heavy mood. They continued to discuss as they sent out a summons.

Thirty minutes later, Knight Commander Albert Hawke and Grand Magus Yuri Drewes were summoned to the king's office. They took their seats as the prime minister explained their intention to dispatch the Third Order to Klausner's Domain.

Both must have predicted this outcome, as neither showed any reaction to this declaration. However, one of Albert's eyebrows twitched when the prime minister implied the existence of another miasma swamp.

Despite the flicker in Albert's expression, Yuri's usual smile remained plastered on his face as he asked, "Will you be sending Lady Sei as well, then?"

"That is correct. She is the only one capable of cleansing the miasma."

The prime minister's words were liable to wound Yuri's pride, as he was a master of magic, but Yuri's expression remained unchanged as he replied with a simple, "Indeed."

Rather, the prime minister was the one whose expression changed when he heard what Yuri had to say next: "However, she herself does not yet possess complete mastery over that power."

"She can't yet use it at will?"

"To put it more precisely, she has been unable to summon it again."

Yuri had submitted an initial report on Sei's lingering inability to call forth those powers. He also had yet to deliver a happy update on the matter, despite the hope that she would manage to sort it out. The prime minister's expression darkened as he realized the situation hadn't changed.

"Since Lady Sei is unable to properly use her powers, would it not be premature to send her to the countryside?" Albert asked in a somewhat stony tone.

Sei hadn't been hurt back in the western forest, but she had been far too close to danger for Albert's comfort—in fact, he was paralyzed with fear by the thought of sending her back into any such situation and loathed the idea of her being exposed to those dangers again.

Not to mention, the Third Order was unfamiliar with the geography of Klausner's Domain, and they wouldn't know precisely what to expect until they got there. It could very well be an even more perilous situation than they had faced in the western forest. In his heart of hearts, Albert had hoped Sei would never be required to go to such a place.

Seeing Albert's worry for Sei, the prime minister touched his chin as he sank into thought. Even if there was a miasma swamp in Klausner's Domain, sending Sei wouldn't solve anything if she couldn't cast the magic.

If sending her would do nothing about the miasma, then it might be better to prioritize her safety and keep her at the palace where they could keep an eye on her.

However, the situation wasn't so simple. While the nobility allied with the palace during national crises, they had their own factions and were far from a monolith. Some nobles cared more for their own interests than those of the kingdom as a whole and, at times, would defy the will of the palace.

Now that the capital was no longer in crisis, if the palace didn't actively support the country nobility, that same nobility was likely to start openly criticizing the government. Furthermore, if the palace proved unwilling to send help when it was most needed, those who had been on the royal family's side would likely rescind future support.

Sending the knights to assist the nobles would likely be enough to appease some of them. Their help might only be a stopgap, but it would nevertheless lead to an overall decrease in the local monster population. However, the houses less inclined to look favorably on the palace wouldn't be satisfied with a temporary solution.

The question, in this case, was whether the nobility was already aware of the Saint's particular ability to defeat monsters.

The prime minister obviously wished that the knights alone could solve the problem, but even their work would take time to accomplish, and no matter how many monsters they slew, they couldn't resolve the likely matter of the multiple swamps. For those, they needed the Saint.

If they could be more certain in their ability to deploy the Saint's powers, then it went without saying that not only would this problem be solved, it would be solved quickly. The events in the western forest were solid proof of that.

However...

The prime minister looked back up and broke the silence. "No, I think she must go."

"Even though she cannot yet call on her powers?" Albert asked.

"It's no longer a matter of whether she can."

Albert gave the prime minister a stern look as the prime minister explained his reasoning. "What's important is that she, the *Saint herself*, shows her support by her presence. If we fail to send her merely because her control of her power is incomplete, the lords of each region will grow agitated."

Albert furrowed his brow. "So you say, but if she can't cleanse the miasma, how can it really make a difference whether she goes or not?"

"What we know is that she has been unable to use her power since her return to the palace. However...what if the issue is that she hasn't been driven by necessity?"

Albert grew silent.

There were still far too many things that they didn't know about Sei's powers and far too few that they did.

Worse, the prime minister might very well be right. Albert had also entertained the possibility that Sei couldn't use her purification magic in the palace because, simply put, she had nothing to purify.

Admittedly, there was also the incident of her herb enhancement at the research institute to factor in, but the prime minister was willing to believe that, in that event, Sei might have used a different power than the one she had deployed against the miasma.

In the end, it still wasn't clear what the Saint needed in order to trigger her powers.

The prime minister recognized that sending Sei anywhere was a gamble, as they had no guarantee she would be able to use her purifying powers once she reached Klausner's Domain. Despite that, when considering all the factors at play, they had no choice *but* to send her.

While Albert understood the needs of the situation, he railed against the notion of sending Sei into the field without greater mastery of her gifts. Without her purifying power, the monsters would linger and in great numbers, even with his knights on hand to handle things. Albert predicted it would take a great deal of time before they could get things under control again, which would surely lead to more criticism from the nobles—especially if they knew the Saint had been present but had done nothing.

It wasn't so much criticism toward the Third Order Albert was worried about, though—he was sure Sei would receive the brunt of it.

His mind reeled, summoning a litany of terrible happenstances one after another, leaving him deeply apprehensive about bringing Sei to Klausner's Domain under these far from perfect conditions.

Albert was about to protest further when the king, who had been silent up until then, finally spoke. "We shall send Lady Sei to Klausner's Domain."

It was the voice of utter authority.

Albert doubted he would win against the king. He clenched his fist and swallowed the words he had been about to say.

The king's decision was the final say at this juncture. Albert resolved himself to return later to make his appeals—he would come with support, and he wouldn't back down.

For the time being, he left the king's office alongside Yuri.

The Saint's
Magic Power is
Omnipotent

ACT

2

Klausner's Domain

"**S**EI."

I heard someone call my name outside the carriage. When I looked out the window, I spotted Albert riding up on a horse.

Albert nodded ahead and said, "We can see it now."

I poked my head a bit out the window and found that down the forested road we could just see a castle on a hill. At the foot of the hill was a town surrounded by high walls. This was the capital of Klausner's Domain.

It was early afternoon, and the sun's rays slanted to the west, making the orange tiled roofs of the houses glint brightly. The dark stone of the castle and protective walls contrasted with these glowing roofs. However, it all looked distinctly European to me, and seeing as I had wanted to visit that part of my old world so badly, the mere sight of it made me let out a gleeful, "Wow!"

You might be thinking: Hey, didn't the capital look just like this? Well, sure, kind of—but this town looked *just* different enough from the capital that I was excited all over again.

The carriage rolled on while I drank in the sights. We proceeded in a line out of the forest and approached a wide-open field of cultivated wheat.

We were almost at our destination.

We had pretty much headed straight here since we left. It only made sense to rush, considering the crisis at hand. However, seeing that our company of knights was, in a word, huge, we couldn't really "rush," per se. It had already taken several days to arrive, and we had stopped in towns along the way, too.

Those pit stops had brought their own problems. Klausner's Domain wasn't the only region experiencing problems—every lord of every territory desperately wanted the palace's aid. Therefore, at every town we'd visited, the lord of the land had come to request our help with all sorts of things. My heart broke a little every time we had to turn them down, but we were in a hurry, and the majority of the requests went beyond our ability to fulfill.

Most of the lords understood the gravity of our responsibilities, but some refused to back down with grace.

It was hard. With respect to the intricacy of political hierarchy, it wasn't like I could just decide to go help them on my own, so I was really at a loss for what to do. I felt absolutely wretched every time I had to decline, and having to do so over and over again weighed on me.

I tried not to let it show on my face, but Albert saw right through me. He didn't say anything about it, but I noticed that he made sure we stopped staying in the capitals and stuck to less important towns.

While I reflected on our trip, we passed through the field and finally arrived at the castle gate. The carriage slowed, adopting a pace more appropriate for town.

Thanks to the vanguard announcing our imminent arrival, we weren't stopped and were permitted to proceed all the way to Lord Klausner's castle.

The town looked more compact than the capital, but it was lovely in its own way. I had assumed the infestation of monsters and the meager herb harvest would have left the town in a dark mood, but it didn't feel that way at all. In fact, the people we passed seemed quite cheerful.

Maybe the situation isn't as bad as we thought? Or maybe the folks out here are made of mentally firmer stuff?

As I wondered, we arrived at the castle entrance, and the carriage came to a stop.

I took a deep breath and gathered my resolve. Starting now, I had to act as the Saint. I waited inside the carriage as I had been instructed beforehand, waiting for someone to open it. I had been told that proper nobles didn't just get out of carriages on their own.

A few moments later, the door opened and light streamed in. I peeked out the door to see Albert standing just outside, his hand outstretched. Although I had been taking courses on etiquette, I still wasn't used to being escorted like this, so I felt a bit shy. In an oddly indescribable state of mind, I smiled awkwardly.

Yeah, best to just smile and make it look like I'm totally cool with this.

I tried my best not to make a weird face as I tentatively took his hand and descended.

When I looked up from my feet, I found a number of servants lined up in front of the castle entrance. Directly in the middle of all of them stood a man clad in elegant attire who looked to be in his late fifties. Strands of gray peppered his hair, and he looked a bit taller than me. *Is he Lord Klausner?*

Albert guided me forward until we stood next to each other before the man.

"I bid you welcome. I am Daniel Klausner, and I govern this land." Lord Klausner bowed gracefully as he introduced himself. The servants behind him simultaneously bowed as well.

Between the lord of a Salutanian domain and the Saint, the Saint won out hands down in terms of status. Although I knew that was the way of it, it felt scathingly awkward to have people pay such respect to me. I was a commoner, born and bred, and I still considered myself as such. I prayed these formalities would be over and done with as soon as possible.

Nevertheless, I forced myself to smile as I greeted him in turn. "I am Sei Takanashi. I look forward to my stay in your domain."

"And I am Albert Hawke, knight commander of the Knights of the Third Order. Pleased to make your acquaintance."

Lord Klausner raised his head only after Albert introduced himself. He then introduced the butler and head maid as the representatives of his servants. Both of them looked to be in their fifties as well. The butler was tall and slender while the head maid was plump and shorter than me. We were to call upon them if we needed anything. I was relieved that they seemed kind and easy to talk to.

"You must be exhausted after such a long journey. First, let us show you to your quarters. Discussions about my domain can wait until after you've had some rest."

"Thank you for your consideration."

Once the introductions were finished, we were shown to our rooms. I was genuinely grateful for this kindness, since I had been cooped up in a carriage all day—although we *had* taken a couple of breaks along the way.

The head maid showed me to my chambers, so I followed her. I was being put up on a higher floor, and in a world without elevators, that meant stairs. So, so many stairs. And yet...

It shocked me to realize how used to climbing I had become over the past year. The palace was quite tall, and it had a ton of long, long staircases. Thanks to those, I now climbed stairs effortlessly—even up distances for which I would have definitely depended on an elevator back in Japan.

At length, we arrived at my quarters. The head maid opened the door to a spacious room full of sunlight. Most of the furniture looked antique and had a subdued color. It was probably made of walnut? The wallpaper and curtains were a matching emerald green. All in all, it was gorgeous.

"These shall be your quarters during your stay."

"Gosh... Thank you."

The head maid no doubt had a boatload of things to do, because she excused herself. For my part, I immediately flopped down on the sofa, leaned back, and stretched.

I realize my behavior was a bit rude, but please forgive me. I was downright pooped after my first long journey in Salutania.

"Would you like to change into your regular attire?" asked Mary, the maid the palace had assigned to wait on me.

"Hmm, I'm going to be seeing Lord Klausner soon, right?"

"I believe so."

"Then shouldn't I just stay in these clothes?"

"You will have to change for your meeting, but perhaps you would like to wear something more comfortable in the meantime."

"Ah, is that so? Well, then."

Mary had come with me since it was possible we'd be here for a while. I could handle daily life necessities on my own, but I was still more or less ignorant of the rules of noble society, even with all my etiquette training. For example, all the intricate little details about what kind of clothes were appropriate for a meeting with a lord? Utterly beyond me. Therefore, Mary was here to help wrestle that sort of situation.

My public image was part of it, too. It would have been a problem for the palace if word got out that the Saint wasn't being waited on. Consequently, another maid had come with Mary as well.

While the other maid put away the luggage I had brought, Mary pulled out my usual clothes. I shucked my current robe with a sense of relief. It was the same fancy get-up I had worn for my audience with the king.

For most of the journey, I had worn my regular clothes and the robes mages of the Royal Magi Assembly preferred, but today I'd had to don the fancy one for the initial meeting with Lord Klausner. Since it wasn't a dress, it wasn't tight or anything, but it wasn't nearly as comfortable as my everyday clothes.

Wait a minute...

"You mean I'm not going to be wearing this robe when I see Lord Klausner later?" I asked, suddenly beset by images of corsets.

"We have another robe selected for you, but if you would rather we prepare a dress..."

I panicked like a kid who'd accidentally reminded their teacher about a homework assignment. "No, no, thanks! The robe sounds great!"

"Very well." Mary and the other maid giggled.

They were both well aware of my dislike for dresses.

But how was I supposed to feel, huh? I wasn't used to wearing them. And frankly, I didn't plan on getting used to them, either.

While I changed into my regular clothes, the other maid showed me the robe I would be wearing later. This one was fantastically elaborate, too. It was a striking sapphire blue with detailed embroidery using a whole rainbow's worth of different-colored threads.

According to Mary, they had brought several dresses, too. At that, I got a bit nervous—not just at the prospect of being stuffed into them, either. Was it really okay for them to lug all these extravagant clothes across the countryside just for me?

"Think nothing of it. This manner of dress is expected of the Saint," the maid said, reading my troubled expression.

"Really?"

"Quite. And just between you and me," the maid dropped her voice, "Lady Aira has several dresses just like these."

"Huh?"

"She received them as gifts from Prince Kyle."

Did she now? I thought—at which point I noticed Mary looming behind the maid with a frightening look on her face.

"Just what are you two talking about?" she asked.

"Oh!" The maid looked like she had been caught saying something inappropriate. She had meant for it to go unheard, but Mary had cottoned on regardless. The maid would be firmly reprimanded later.

After I got changed, I chatted with the two of them, but soon, there was a knock at the door. Mary opened it to find the head maid we had met before. She had brought some tea for us to enjoy.

"Thank you," I said to her as she set the tea on the table in front of the sofa.

She smiled brightly at me before she left. "You are quite welcome. I hope everything is to your satisfaction and that you have been able to relax."

Mary took over pouring the tea, which had a faint and lovely hue. I raised it to my lips for a sip. It had a unique perfume, likely from some naturally fragrant herb. Frankly, that just made sense given we were in Klausner's Domain.

Hm...this is a bit nostalgic, actually. Maybe from Japan? What herb is it, though? I reached for an apple that had been brought to accompany the tea. It was smaller than the ones I remembered back home, and as I took a bite, I found the texture crisp and the flavor as refreshingly sweet as it was sour.

Sweet foods are perfect for recovering from fatigue.

Time passed in the blink of an eye as I took it easy, chatting with Mary and the other maid. Eventually, I realized that the sun had dipped and shadows lined the window.

Wait, what about my meeting with Lord Klausner?

When I asked Mary, she said, "I did not hear a specific time. Shall I go find out?"

"Yes, please."

Just then, there was another knock at the door. One of the castle maids had come by. I caught bits and pieces of her conversation with Mary, but it sounded like it wasn't what I was expecting. In fact, Mary reported that it wasn't about any official kind of meeting at all.

"I'm having dinner with Lord Klausner's family?" I blinked.

"Yes. She didn't say anything about the discussions, either."

"I see."

Well, this just felt odd. But maybe we would discuss the state of things over a meal.

For now it was time to get ready—and at least I had Mary to help me deal with this change of plans.

A castle maid led me to the dining room.

I was leaving behind a bit of a dispute. A dispute about what? My wardrobe. Just a slight difference of opinion, really!

It was considered a given that the nobles of Salutania wore ornate gowns to dinner. Therefore, Mary had quickly selected one, but I had insisted on wearing the sapphire robe she had shown me earlier. Why? Because I was totally exhausted, duh! I was *not* in the mood for such constricting clothing.

As a woman who'd never been popular with men, I didn't aspire to sparkly, frilly dresses. That being said, the popular fashion in Salutania trended extravagant and awe-inspiring—even a glimpse of any of their gowns made my heart race. And I'd always liked looking at cute clothes back in Japan... But, well, I didn't think any of these pretty things particularly suited me. A part of me sometimes wished it were different, but I always felt guilty putting on anything I had no business wearing.

When I first came to this world, I had been a tad excited about wearing fancy dresses, since I was obligated to—which meant I wouldn't have to feel guilty for doing so. However, the first time I actually wore one of them, I realized the sharp difference between imagination and reality. It was fun to look at these dresses, but wearing them all day was wickedly painful, especially the corsets.

Uncomfortable at the best of times, I felt a corset would be the end of me in my current state. And anyway, I doubted I could actually eat if my waist were being squeezed.

Let me tell you, I was relieved I'd managed to convince the maids to let me wear the robe.

"Sei."

"Lord Hawke."

Albert called for my attention as soon as I entered the dining hall. He had changed out of his traveling attire as well and wore a standard knight's uniform.

"Is that a new robe?" he asked.

"Yes. I guess the palace had it made for me."

"I see. It looks wonderful on you."

Oh, come on! That bomb left me absolutely shaken. I usually wore the same outfit all the time, so I still didn't have any resistance against being praised for my fashion sense.

"Huh? Oh, uh, th-thank you," I managed, my cheeks burning.

Meanwhile, he wore that alluring, handsome smile of his. It was good manners to compliment a woman's attire, but was it all right for me to compliment him back?

Like for example, "And you look as unbelievably hot as always!"

Ha, as if I had the courage!

"Shall we go?" He offered me his arm.

"R-right." My heart pounded as I took it.

Within the dining hall, we found Lord Klausner's family already seated. It appeared we were the last to arrive. We took our seats, Lord Klausner greeted us, and the dinner began.

As I listened to Lord Klausner's welcoming speech, I remembered something unpleasant: the state of the cooking in this country.

I had completely forgotten about that little issue because I was used to eating meals of my own devising at the institute. Suffice to say, the cuisine in this country was lacking in the seasoning department. In other words, the food was flavor-challenged. This shortcoming became especially obvious in fancier dishes. Fruits and veggies were generally okay since they had their own sweet or sour flavors, but dishes with meat uniformly left something to be desired.

I was famished, but I started grimly wondering whether I should've worn a dress after all, as I wasn't likely to enjoy this meal. Squeezing my stomach with a corset would probably have made me feel full faster.

Dang it, I thought as the dishes were brought out. But as I examined them, I let out a soft, "Oh…"

Lord Klausner smiled at my surprise, but my attention was more fixed on the food: roast chicken, a common enough Salutanian dish, but this bird was garnished with rosemary—a combination I remembered from my old world.

The butler began slicing the chicken, which had been roasted whole. A delicious smell wafted up from it. When I took a bite of the serving put on my plate, my mouth was filled with not only the flavor of rosemary but other herbs.

"How do you like it?" Lord Klausner asked.

"It's heavenly. Is this a local recipe?"

"Actually, no. I simply heard using herbs in this particular way had become popular in the palace, so I decided to give it a try."

Knowingly or not, he was referring to my own recipes. However, this dish used a far more complex combination of herbs than I typically did. Perhaps the chef had added them in? They had to have a deep knowledge of flavors—just as one would expect of someone who grew up in a domain known for its herbal variety.

In any case, the chefs I taught my recipes to had passed their knowledge on to the other chefs in the palace, and as a result, knowledge of these dishes—which were rather popular, if I do say so myself—had continued to spread. If the people who got to try those dishes at the palace dining hall were in turn sharing the recipes with the country nobility, maybe I wouldn't have to worry about bland meals as we traveled. Frankly, I hoped everyone's cooking started leveling up.

Seriously, though. First that striking herb tea, now this delicious chicken. I was already impressed by Klausner's Domain.

As we ate, Lord Klausner told me more about the region, describing not only the current state of things but the land itself.

Since their territory's main industry was the cultivation of medicinal herbs, naturally they were a big focus. We discussed the kinds of herbs they grew and those that could be picked around the town, all of which was of great interest to me. Lord Klausner even brought up herbs I hadn't ever heard of, and I couldn't help asking him question after question. Fortunately, he didn't show any outward sign of displeasure, and he answered everything I put to him.

"I heard you make potions as well, is that correct?" he asked.

"I do," I said. "I usually work at the Research Institute of Medicinal Flora."

"I see. Then you must be a competent alchemist as well."

"I'm not sure I would say my skills are *alchemist*-level good..."

"We have our own practitioners here in the castle, you know."

"You do?"

According to Lord Klausner, the castle alchemists were known as the greatest in the kingdom. I was sure this wasn't an exaggeration—you had to be good indeed if you were going to be so well regarded in the so-called alchemist's holy land.

Then I remembered Liz telling me about the secret potion recipes the domain's alchemists were said to pass down in their families. Such great alchemists would surely know about that sort of thing. It might be hard to get them to share any particular recipes with me, but I hoped they would be willing to at least teach me more about regular potions and herbs.

I asked Lord Klausner if I could meet them, and he readily agreed. In fact, it seemed he had predicted my interest. The conversation moved quickly, and Lord Klausner assured me that during my stay, we would definitely be introduced.

Just as he made this promise, the dinner came to an end.

I had a pretty nice time getting to talk about this powerful interest of mine. However, we hadn't discussed the state of the domain at all. I was so absorbed in the herb-talk that I completely forgot to ask about it. *I suppose that's a problem for tomorrow-Sei...*

"What's wrong?" Albert asked, frowning at me as I walked in contemplative silence. He was escorting me back to my room.

"I forgot to ask about the monsters, is all."

"Ah, well, don't worry about that. I already got the details."

"You did?"

According to Albert, he had spoken to Lord Klausner and someone from the mercenary company while I was relaxing in my quarters. They hadn't summoned me to join them because they figured I would be exhausted from my first long journey. I was thankful, sure, but I felt guilty that I hadn't been part of it—this was my job, after all.

"Will you be heading out on an expedition right away?" I asked.

"No, we'll take a few days to do some preliminary scouting. You should wait here in the castle."

"All right."

I asked because I assumed they would need me to join whenever they set out in earnest. Scouting made sense, though. They'd need to figure out the lay of the land and what kind of monsters we'd be up against.

But if I was going to wait around here in the castle, then maybe I could meet with those alchemists right away.

Oh, yeah. I should ask if I can make extra potions here, too. I had brought some from the palace, but ideally, I would get to replenish them here. There was an herb shortage in the capital, but I imagined there might still be some available in the domain of their origin. I would have to ask Lord Klausner about it tomorrow.

And so, Albert and I discussed our plans for the next day as I headed back to my chamber.

The following morning, I ate breakfast with Lord Klausner and his family in a different dining hall, one that was considerably smaller.

When I asked, he promised to introduce me to the castle's head alchemist once we were finished. The alchemist worked full-time in a place called the brewery, where all the castle's potions were made.

After breakfast, Lord Klausner guided me down the hallway to the brewery, which was on the first floor of the castle. When we arrived, Lord Klausner knocked on the door before opening it.

As we went inside, I caught a whiff of herbs. Against the walls were several shelves packed with bottles of dried herbs and tools for making potions. A table in the center of the room was covered with even more apparatuses. On the opposite side, it seemed there was an entrance to a back room.

Several people were working away. Although they noticed Lord Klausner come in, all they did was give him a slight bow and continue whatever they were doing. Lord Klausner didn't say anything about it, so this attitude seemed normal to all of them.

I tilted my head, wondering which of these people we were looking for. Lord Klausner headed over to the back room and called, "Corinna."

"Oh, if it isn't the master of the castle. What can I do for you?" answered an old woman with white hair as she emerged from the back. She was a bit hunched, and shorter than even the head maid. Because of that, while she didn't look fat or anything, she gave off the impression of being very small and round. Despite that—and her age—she gave off a sense of vigor and professionalism.

"This is the Saint, Lady Takanashi, who has arrived from the capital."

"Um, hi—my name is Sei Takanashi."

"It is a pleasure to meet you. I am Corinna, an alchemist in this castle."

I had mixed feelings about being introduced as "the Saint," but I knew it couldn't be avoided. I accidentally wound up letting my awkwardness show with a stiff smile. However, Corinna paid it no mind.

After the introductions, Corinna gave Lord Klausner a look as if to ask why he'd interrupted her workday.

"Lady Takanashi also brews potions. She expressed an interest in meeting you."

"Is that so?"

"Um, if it's all right with you, I was hoping to hear more about your expertise?" I asked.

"I don't mind at all. I was just about to start making today's batch, actually. How about we chat while I work on them?"

"Yes, please!" I thanked my lucky stars for this opportunity to watch a great alchemist at work. I was sure to learn something from her.

Lord Klausner had other business to attend to, so he left us in the brewery. As he did, Corinna went to gather some herbs off the shelves.

"Are you going to make mid-grade HP potions?" I asked.

"Yes, that's right. You do know your stuff, don't you?"

"Oh, I just happened to remember—I make mid-grade potions pretty frequently."

At my mention of "frequently," I could have sworn I caught a glint in Corinna's eye. Maybe it was just my imagination.

I watched her closely as she set to work with a serious expression on her face. She was quite skillful, just as I expected.

As she worked, Corinna talked me through each of the herbs she was using and the potions they might go into, her deft hands never faltering. She made one potion after another, and just as she finished the fifth, she sighed. She seemed somewhat tired.

Oh, that's right. Normal alchemists can only make about ten mid-grade potions a day. I keep forgetting. I'd never had to deal with the same limitation, after all. It also occurred to me that Corinna really did have to be quite skilled in order to make five in a row.

"Would you like to make some as well?" Corinna offered.

"May I?"

I was just a guest who she had met mere minutes before. Was she really comfortable letting me borrow her place of work? Or maybe she was going to offer to teach me? When I asked, she responded with a smile and nod.

I was excited at the prospect of her mentorship and got to work making potions like I usually did. Now it was Corinna's turn to watch how I worked.

One potion, two potions, three potions...

Corinna didn't say a word as I made one potion after another. Was my process okay? I wasn't about to ask if she wasn't going to say anything first, but I started to get a bit uneasy.

Six potions, seven potions, eight potions...

She still wasn't stopping me, so I kept on at it.

Just as I started on my tenth, her expression changed.

"You can keep going?" Corinna asked as she watched me, visibly shocked.

"Yes, I usually make many more than this a day."

"Aha. Well, I suppose it shouldn't be any surprise." Corinna let out an astonished laugh.

Maybe I should've stopped with five? I chuckled awkwardly.

Corinna kept a smile on her face as she said, "It's just that when I heard the Saint herself liked to make potions, I assumed it was just a hobby. But I see now that you're already an expert."

"Uh...thank you."

"I think we'll be able to have far more interesting discussions," she said with a wider grin. My eyes sparkled.

Maybe she'll teach me those secret recipes?

I looked at Corinna with such hope, but she must have guessed what I was thinking because she flatly dismissed that idea. "Don't get ahead of yourself. We start with the basics."

"Yes, ma'am."

Corinna smiled wryly at my slightly disappointed face. "In any case, Lady Takanashi, I'll start with an explanation on the practical uses of low-grade HP potions."

"Okay! But...may I please ask you to not refer to me as 'Lady Takanashi'? Just Sei is fine, especially since I'm the one learning from you."

"Are you sure? Very well, then."

Corinna had already dropped the pretense of polite bearing, so it felt kind of weird to hear her keep addressing me as "Lady" anything. And I knew it was a bit late for me to start acting all polite toward her, but I *was* to be the student, after all.

When I asked her to treat me like she would anyone else, she at least understood that this was more comfortable for me.

We really got into the thick of it after that, and I promptly decided that on days when I didn't have to join an expedition, I would learn about herbs and potions from Corinna while helping her to make her quota.

ACT 3

Mercenaries

ONE MORNING, I set out to make potions as the sun rose. I headed down to the brewery as soon as I got dressed. There, I often found Corinna already busy—she got up incredibly early.

In this world, it was typical to start working at the crack of dawn. I tried to follow that norm as well, but Corinna always seemed to be going at it by the time I caught up with her.

Once I had tried to meet her at the brewery when she got there, but she'd told me not to come until everyone else did. It turned out that she worked on private projects before the brewery opened to everyone else. She wouldn't tell me any details, but I got the impression this work was related to those secret recipes I kept hearing about.

When I arrived at the brewery, Corinna was once more hard at work.

"Good morning," I chirped.

"Oh, good morning, Sei. Could I ask you to prepare some mid-grade HP potions today? I have the quota written on that notepad over there."

"Got it."

Using the notepad as a reference, I put together the necessary ingredients. The herbs I assembled on my work desk were a bit different from the ones I used back at the institute—for one, this recipe required some herbs we didn't typically use, but overall, it had fewer total ingredients. As it turned out, this was Corinna's personal brew.

As I stirred the ingredients in a pot, the door to the room opened with a bang. Although it had been a few hours since we started, it was still pretty early in the morning. I looked at the door in surprise, wondering who the heck would be storming in at such a time.

The man in the door was so tall he could only be described as a giant, and he had a frightening look on his face as he strode into the room.

His height wasn't the only big thing about him. He was also, ah, how should I put it? *Thick*.

The Knights of the Third Order were muscular, sure, but this guy surpassed them in every anatomical regard.

His arms and chest were utterly stacked. He was so huge, his mere presence made the room feel cramped.

His hair was short and brown—a similar color to Johan's, actually, though his seemed a bit dryer. I'd never noticed it before, but it seemed Johan took good care of his hair.

More importantly, this man's amber eyes were terribly sharp. As he surveyed the room, he spotted me and peered. "Hmm? Are you one of Granny's apprentices?"

By "Granny," did he mean Corinna? She *had* been teaching me a ton, and I felt like there was an unspoken agreement that I was something like one of her apprentices, but I wasn't sure if I could make a real claim to the title.

As I was struggling with how to answer, Corinna came out from the back room. "What's all this ruckus first thing in the morning? Can't you be a bit quieter when you come in?"

"Hey, I tried."

"You call that trying?" Corinna sighed. "What do you want?"

"Oh, right, I came here to pick up the potions we ordered yesterday."

"You really think we'd be done with an order you placed last night?"

"Oh, uh, no, of course not, and I'm sorry, but it's just, we've suddenly been summoned...to..." Under Corinna's sharp glare, the man's voice weakened and he trailed off. The way he started faltering made him seem like a dejected dog who had just been scolded. I could almost see his doggy ears drooping.

While Corinna was small, she was a terror when she got angry. This big guy was flinching back from her.

However, I could understand her irritability. We had only received the order he was asking for the prior evening, just when we were finished with work for the day. It had come from a mercenary, though not this man. Also, the mercenary hadn't mentioned a deadline, so we'd been planning to finish the order by this afternoon. In fact, I was working on part of it at that very moment.

It wasn't a problem, though.

"I guess you've left us no choice then. Sei?"

I nodded to Corinna. "On it."

And so, I went into the back room to retrieve a bunch of extra potions from the storage rack. They had asked for quite a number, so the man wore a look of surprise when he saw that we could, in fact, match the order ahead of time. He must not have expected us to actually be done yet.

And, well, usually there wouldn't be any way to have an excess of potions during an herb shortage, buuut... Yup. That was on me.

We'd wound up inadvertently stockpiling them while I was practicing Corinna's secret recipe for mid- and high-grade potions. Of course, I had obtained her permission for this. According to Corinna, "They'll be needed before long anyway."

Thus, we had quite a trove of potions stored away in the brewery in case of emergencies—just like the trove we had back at the Research Institute of Medicinal Flora.

"I knew we could count on you, Granny," said the man.

"Hmph. Sei's the one you should be thanking, not me."

"Sei?"

"She's the one who made all these, but I can vouch for their effectiveness."

The man glanced at me again.

I introduced myself with a bow and a, "Sei, here."

The man strode over to me. "The name's Leonhardt. I'm in charge of this castle's mercenary company."

He held out his right hand to me. I assumed he was asking for a handshake, so I held out mine and he grasped it firmly in his own. He grinned and clapped me on the shoulder. "Pleased to meet ya."

I couldn't help but stagger.

"Leo! You shouldn't be so rough with women!"

"Whoa! Sorry!"

"I-It's all right..."

I stood straight again and glanced up at Leonhardt to find him wearing a nervous expression of panic mixed with regret. Since he apologized so quickly, I was sure he wasn't a bad guy.

"I'm really sorry about that," he said again. "Are you okay?"

"Yes, I'm fine." I smiled.

His expression melted into relief. "Thanks for the potions."

He didn't wait to hear my response as he scooped up the box of potions and swept out the door.

The brewery went silent once more.

That guy sure was energetic. The room seemed even quieter than usual once he was gone.

Early that afternoon, Corinna brought me to one of the vast fields of herbs that grew in the area.

We had passed through a field of wheat when we arrived in Klausner's Domain, but in the opposite direction lay the fields for medicinal herbs. The palace had an enormous herb garden, but these fields were far larger—I wouldn't have expected anything less from this domain.

There was also a forest at the boundary, so I couldn't say the fields extended as far as the eye could see, but they were cultivated all the way up to the forest edge.

The fields were outside the protection of the town walls, but it was safe according to Corinna. Monsters rarely approached the walls, and the ones that did were quite weak. Corinna assured me that if anything dared show itself, she would be able to handle it herself.

In a corner of the great fields, Corinna was giving me another lesson in herbology. In short, we were doing fieldwork. I was squatting down in the middle of a field, listening to her explanation while I studied the plants growing around us.

I actually didn't know anything about the plant I was presently looking at. It might well have been unique to this world. Or, at the very least, it was one I hadn't heard of back when I was getting into aromatherapy and so forth in Japan.

As I examined the specimen, Corinna taught me the identifying characteristics of its appearance, its medicinal benefits, and things to be cautious of when harvesting a sample.

"It doesn't have any special effects on its own, but when mixed with other herbs, it can increase the potency of HP restoration."

"So that's why you can use fewer ingredients when you mix it in with standard recipes."

"Correct."

This was the herb that Corinna used in her secret recipe. I hadn't recognized it at first, as the ones I had used in the potions had already been dried. According to her, since its only effect was catalytic, it generally wasn't recognized as a "medicinal herb," per se.

I see. So it might actually be a plant that exists back in my world, too—it just wouldn't have been in my aromatherapy dictionaries. I got the feeling it hadn't been categorized as an herb in Japan, either.

Corinna finished her explanation, and we stood up to head over to the next patch.

I was stretching out the kinks in my body when I heard a shout from behind. "So this is where you've been!"

I turned in the direction of the unfamiliar voice to find a muscular man loping toward us down the path between the fields. It was Leonhardt, the man I had met just that morning.

I glanced beyond Leonhardt as he rushed toward us, suddenly caught up in a memory of an old friend of mine—she really loved muscles. Like, she was obsessed. *My dear friend, never have I have ever wished you were here more than I do in this moment. I bet you'd think you'd gone to heaven.*

I hoped they forgave me for my faraway, distracted look.

Leonhardt seemed to have just returned from an expedition, because there were a ton of men behind him—his mercenary company, I presumed. Leonhardt possessed a praiseworthy physique, but the others with him had to be commended as well. What would you call these types again? Macho? Every single one of them had that same admirable body type.

If my friend were here, surely she'd be pumping her fist in excitement. As I was thinking such worthless thoughts, Leonhardt finally caught up to us.

The moment he got close enough, he started talking rather animatedly. "Hey, Granny! Were those potions you gave us this morning new?"

"Huh? Why do you say that?"

"They were way more effective than usual!"

"I see. That's nice."

"Yeah, but...so that means they *weren't* new, then? Did you give us high-grade ones by accident?"

"Don't be thick. There's no way we could make that many high-grade potions in these times."

Leonhardt's shoulders drooped at Corinna's curt manner.

By "new," does he mean a new type of potion?

I was pretty sure the potions we'd given them this morning were the ones I'd made while practicing with the secret recipe. Judging from what he was describing, it sounded like my fifty-percent-bonus curse was at it again.

"But there's no way mid-grade potions could have been that effective."

"Yeah, yeah."

The other mercenaries came up from behind Leonhardt and surrounded us, all of them musing over the incredible potency of the new potions.

"Even the low-grade ones were more potent today," said one.

"I don't think they were better than the mid-grade ones, but maybe they were about the same?" said another.

Well how was that for déjà vu?

"Didn't I tell you that I could vouch for their effectiveness?" Corinna said.

"Oh yeah, you weren't the one who made them." Leonhardt suddenly turned toward me. Everyone else followed his gaze as well.

Augh! Again?! I really hated getting ganged up on like this.

As I was at a loss, Corinna swooped to my rescue. "I suppose you could say they're new. Those were indeed mid-grade HP potions we gave you this morning, but they're made from Sei's secret recipe."

"For real?! That's amazing! I can't believe she can make something like that at her age!" Leonhardt perked up and started clapping me on the shoulder again.

"Ow!" I staggered.

"Leo!" Corinna snapped.

I really wish he would learn a little restraint.

I smiled awkwardly as Leonhardt apologized once more, looking deflated. "Sorry."

My secret recipe, huh? I had only included the ingredients Corinna told me to in the potions Leonhardt and his company had been using—the only difference had been my magical power, which I called on to imbue the potions as they were brewed.

My magical power was...unusual. Different from everyone else's, to say the least. And I suppose you could say it was an ingredient, which meant that it did, kind of, sort of, constitute my own secret recipe.

However, true secret recipes required a great deal of effort to design, especially those that were exceptionally potent. Calling what I did *my* secret recipe just because of my inborn powers made me feel kind of pathetic. I mean,

I'd also definitely made the potions using Corinna's recipe as a base.

I surreptitiously glanced Corinna's way. She merely raised an eyebrow and gave me a slight nod. She was probably telling me not to worry about it.

I still felt bad though, so I gave her a slight bow in a subtle way so that Leonhardt and his men wouldn't notice. She just smiled back.

The men didn't notice this exchange, thank goodness. After some more lively discussion, they headed back to the castle.

"Still though, you're amazing. It's great that we have more skilled alchemists here. I hope you'll keep on making those potions for us!" Leonhardt declared.

"Uh, will do."

He was about to pound me on the shoulder again with his goodbye, but he seemed to remember what had happened earlier and stopped at the last second. He looked embarrassed for a moment before putting his raised hand on his head to scratch it.

With that farewell, Leonhardt's lively company headed back to the castle.

I sighed. Corinna patted my back. I glanced over at her to find an exasperated look on her face as she chuckled. "Let's head to the next spot."

"Okay."

At her encouragement, we headed to the next patch of unusual herbs.

◆ ◆ ◆

I reached a good stopping place for my work, said my goodbyes to everyone in the brewery, and went out into the hallway. As I was heading back to my quarters, I spotted Albert coming toward me from the opposite direction.

"Lord Hawke."

"Sei. I'm glad I found you. I was looking everywhere."

"You were?"

He'd come to the brewery specifically to meet up with me.

"Did something happen?" I asked.

"Not as such, but I wanted to tell you a bit about our initial survey."

"Sure—should we go now?"

"Yes. Let's go to the quarters reserved for the Third Order."

We gave each other some general life updates and other small talk as we made our way to our destination. I told him about everything I was learning in the brewery from Corinna and the other alchemists—stuff I couldn't learn anywhere else.

Because Lord Klausner had introduced me as the Saint, everyone had kept a respectful distance from me at first, but they'd warmed up to me once they heard me asking Corinna a nonstop slew of questions. Or maybe it would be more accurate to say they were as interested in me as I was in them because of my work at the Research Institute of Medicinal Flora. The first time one of them talked to me, she reminded me of Yuri when he went on one of his wild magic tangents.

And it wasn't just her, either. As you'd expect from a place referred to as a holy land, everyone in the brewery was passionate about herbology, and all of them got that light in their eyes whenever we really dug into the topic.

That first was just the start—as we talked, gradually more and more people had joined our circle.

They had all sorts of questions, mostly about what herbs the institute was presently studying or if we were working on any new recipes. I could only answer with information from our official publications—ongoing research was kept private—but it took so long for any new info to get to Klausner's Domain from the capital that there were plenty of things they hadn't heard about yet. They thanked me heartily for the updates. I was just happy to help.

Things got really exciting when I brought up using herbs in cooking—my new friends were over the moon with delighted interest, just like Johan had been when I first told him about medicinal cooking.

Corinna was especially interested in these medicinal dishes, and she asked me a ton of questions. She was interested in trying some of them, but unfortunately, I didn't know any recipes. Therefore, I could only talk about the meals I made at the capital and the effects of the herbs I used. Granted, that alone was enough to garner everyone's undivided attention.

During these exchanges, I became quite well acquainted with everyone who worked in the brewery. And, of course, I got to ask my share of questions, too. Some folks were even willing to share their secret recipes with me, and overall I learned a ton of things that sounded like they would be useful for my future research. I was terribly grateful to all of them.

"It sounds like working at the brewery has been a good experience for you," Albert said.

"It really has!"

"I'm glad you seem to be enjoying yourself."

"Oh, uh, um..."

He laughed, and I glanced up to find him looking at me with a gentle expression. I supposed I'd gotten a bit enthusiastic, even though I was talking about such dry, technical things as herbs and potions that Albert didn't know the first thing about.

I felt a bit, how do you say, mortified, and my cheeks started to glow. I looked down reflexively and heard him chuckle again.

When we arrived at the quarters for the Third Order, I discovered that "quarters" actually meant "entire two-story building" on the castle grounds. Albert explained that the knightly Orders always stayed in this building while visiting Klausner's Domain.

The first floor was a waiting room, so the building opened up into a spacious hall as soon as we went inside. A bunch of knights were gathered around a long table, where they were discussing a map laid across it.

I was acquainted with all of them, so when they noticed Albert and I enter the room, they waved casually in greeting. I followed Albert through the great hall and up the stairs in the back. The second floor was divided into several quarters, and Albert was using one of them as his office. Inside was a desk and two sofas, just like in his office back at the palace barracks. At his prompting, we sat facing one another.

"Let's jump right in, then," he said.

"Of course."

Albert launched right in without any further preamble. The knights had been split into several squads for the survey. They had explored all four cardinal directions in rotation as they scouted the periphery. The knights we passed downstairs had just returned from their own sally.

As they scouted, they were slaying any monsters they came across. According to the reports, there were as many monsters here as there had been around the capital, pre-swamp-purification. Once the knights completed their scouting, they would begin undertaking full-scale monster-slaying expeditions, but they expected it would take some time for things to become stable.

Albert agreed with this assessment. "I really wish I could get you back to the palace sooner rather than later, but unfortunately...I expect it will take time."

"Don't you worry about me. I've been learning a ton."

"I see." His apologetic look turned to one of relief. Then he smiled—perhaps remembering how enthusiastic I'd been just minutes ago.

Ack. Sorry I'm so crazy about potions. Thinking that reminded me of something. "If you've been running into monsters during your surveys, then that means you've been using potions, right?"

"That's right."

"How's your supply?"

"We have the stores we brought from the capital, but if we run out, I'm planning to buy some here in town."

"Um. Wouldn't you like me to make them?"

"You?"

"Yeah. Of course, I'll need you to get me the ingredients, but I think it'll be cheaper to buy the herbs than it would be to buy the potions themselves."

"But don't you need your equipment?"

"Well… I was thinking of asking Lord Klausner if I could use the brewery for this exact purpose."

"I see. Then I'll go ahead and request permission for you."

"Please! Thank you."

While the knights continued to scout, they wouldn't need all that many potions—hopefully. But once we started going on full-fledged expeditions, the consumption rate would increase substantially. Considering how many knights were going with us, I imagined I'd be at work for a while.

Fortunately, I now knew Corinna's secret recipe, so I would be able to conserve the amount of ingredients I needed to meet demand. Even the local town suffered a bit from the overall herb shortage, after all. Also, it *did* make more economic sense for me to do it…

And, I admit, I just kind of wanted the excuse to practice. Although I had Corinna's permission to do so,

I'd been trying not to go too overboard for the sake of discretion. I kept having flashbacks to the lines and lines of potions I'd left behind at the institute.

However, if I was going to supply both the mercenary company and the Third Order, then surely it would be okay to get diligent and make a few more.

"Actually—one thing, about the expeditions," I said.

"What about them?"

"Will the mercenaries be going with you?"

Albert gave me an odd look.

What's with him?

He thought his answer over for a bit before giving an evasive reply.

The day we had arrived in Klausner's Domain, Albert and his knights had received the report on the monster situation while I idled in my chamber. At that time, Albert had met the leader of the mercenary company, but it sounded like they hadn't really meshed well.

The mercenary company that protected Klausner's Domain was well known for its brawn and bravado, so they had rarely asked the Orders for assistance. However, the knights were necessary this time, given the severity of the issue and its far-reaching impact.

Nevertheless, the company probably took pride in their work, even if they defended the land for pay rather than out of some honorable calling. I could see why they might be reluctant to work with the knights—I had heard they only went to the initial meeting because Lord Klausner told them to.

In any case, even though the knights and mercenaries were working in tandem, they weren't acting *together*. Instead, they split up their groups and visited different allotted zones to slay monsters.

Now that I thought about it, the guy Albert met in his meeting with Lord Klausner might have been Leonhardt. Hadn't he mentioned he was in charge of the company when we first met?

At the time, he hadn't seemed like the kind of person to give people the cold shoulder just because they were from the capital or anything. *Then again, what did he really know about me? He only ever got my name.*

Albert interrupted my thoughts. "Something the matter?"

"Was Leonhardt the mercenary you met?"

"Yes... You know him?"

"I met him this morning—in the brewery. He came to pick up some potions."

"I see. Did he say anything about all this to you?"

"No, not at all."

Leonhardt thought I was Corinna's apprentice, so

Albert had nothing to worry about there. But there was always the possibility Leonhardt would find out I'd come here with the Third Order.

I wasn't too worried about that, though. I had met the mercenaries in the field just hours ago, and they had been so good-natured. Even though I'd had my reservations about them at first, I could tell I was starting to warm up to them. Maybe that was a bit too optimistic of me?

"Don't worry about Leonhardt—I like him," I said. "Anyway, when do you think the expeditions will start?"

"Tomorrow we'll be scouting again, but I'll be sure to let you know when we change tack."

"Sounds good."

Guess I won't be needed for a little while yet. In that case, I'll do a bit more studying before I start prep—oh, and I should probably tell Corinna we might be selling potions to the Order, huh?

As I started putting together my plans in my head for the next few days, I said goodbye to Albert and at last returned to my quarters.

Behind the Scenes II

THREE MEN SAT facing each other on the sofas in Lord Klausner's office: Lord Daniel Klausner, Albert, and Leonhardt.

Daniel introduced the other two. "This is Leonhardt, the leader of the mercenary company I employ. And this is Lord Albert Hawke, the knight commander of the Knights of the Third Order, sent by the palace to lend us aid."

Leonhardt wordlessly bowed his head. He demonstrated the appropriate deference toward a noble, but something of an aggressive glint flickered in his eye.

Albert noticed this, but he responded with a placid nod, his facial expression showing no hint of tension.

As the head of a mercenary company, Leonhardt had to deal with nobles far more often than his men did.

Therefore, he knew how to handle himself in these situations. His rough exterior also concealed a keen mind. He understood the gravity of the current situation and had viewed his lord's request for knightly aid as inevitable. However, that didn't mean he was entirely at peace with the situation.

Leonhardt and his men were proud of the effort they had shown up until this point. Moreover, they were having trouble viewing the Third Order as anything but outsiders, even though some had tried to reconcile with the idea of help from the capital. Fundamentally, it was a problem of pride.

With the introductions over, Daniel launched into a rundown of the current situation. It wasn't that he didn't notice Leonhardt's discomfort, he just wanted to hurry the conversation along in a businesslike manner and get it over with before anyone got too tense.

"So there *has* been an increase in monsters?" Albert asked.

"I'm afraid so. The forest is full of them, and we've seen them breach the forest perimeter more and more frequently. However, the mercenary company takes care of any of those who stray past the tree line."

"But the ones within must still be seen to."

"Exactly."

"Then please, send us to take care of those."

Leonhardt, who had been silent, chose then to speak up. "Wouldn't it be better if we took care of the forest while you guys take over stray duty? You and your lot only just got here. You don't know the lay of the land."

Albert gently vetoed Leonhardt's proposal. "Your mercenaries are indeed more knowledgeable about the local geography. However, I believe it will be necessary for us to enter the forest in order to most accurately grasp the nature of the situation."

Albert wanted to avoid conflict with the mercenaries, so he tried to deliver his counterplan with grace. After all, he couldn't back down on this: based on the state of things, the palace had concluded that a black swamp was located somewhere in Klausner's Domain, just like the one that had been in Ghoshe Forest. Furthermore, this hypothetical swamp was most likely within the forest, as miasma tended to coalesce in such areas.

If there really was a black swamp, it would be beyond the mercenary company's ability to handle. Albert could easily imagine a disastrous outcome in such a confrontation, given his experiences with the swamp in the western forest.

"I heard the Saint traveled with you. Is there a reason she isn't present?" Leonhardt asked.

"We're letting her rest in her quarters. She was exhausted," Albert said.

"But you're bringing the Saint on your expeditions, yes? You make it sound like she's got poor endurance. You sure you should send her into the forest?"

"It will be fine. She is merely unaccustomed to long journeys. We won't be going on an expedition for a few days yet, either. Please know that she joined us on just such an expedition into Ghoshe Forest."

"You mean that one west of the capital? She really went in there?"

"Of course. She fought with us until the end."

"Well, then."

Though Albert was a bit surprised that Leonhardt knew of the Saint's presence, the truth was that over the past few days, the people of Klausner's castle had been in a tizzy preparing for her arrival. As news went, it would've been hard to miss.

Albert was also impressed that, for all of his dislike of the Third Order's presence, Leonhardt simply confirmed the Saint's well-being and competence before immediately backing down. He had thought the man would be more stubborn—more brusque.

This assumption of Albert's was based on prior experience, back in the days he had been able to leave the capital to aid country lords with monstrous incursions. Back then, most mercenary companies had done their damnedest to send the knightly Orders packing, regardless of whether the knights had come at the behest of the lord of the domain.

This resentment was, unfortunately, also based in experience. Every mercenary had their reasons for taking up the work, but most commonly, they needed the money. However, some lords used the presence of knights as an excuse to decrease how much they paid their mercenaries. Although in such cases the lord was to blame, the mercenaries could only take out their anger on the knights. In that sense, Leonhardt's composure likely had something to do with Daniel's excellent treatment of his company.

Albert hoped this meant they might even be able to build a relationship with mutual trust. They didn't have to like each other; so long as they could discuss business with cool heads, they wouldn't have any problems.

If there was any potential for friction, it came down to the question of what kind of attitude Leonhardt would take toward the Saint.

As someone who put her all into her work, Sei would no doubt be able to do her job even if the mercenaries resented her for her association with the knights. But that didn't mean she wouldn't be hurt. Albert wanted more than anything to relieve Sei of as much pain as possible.

I'll have to do what I can to limit contact between the mercenaries and the Saint. I won't let Sei be exposed to their discontent. That was what Albert decided in his heart.

The mercenary company had their own quarters in Klausner's castle. They went out on their rounds every day, but they spent the rest of their time on standby in these rooms. While on standby, they maintained their gear, chatted, and spent their time as they pleased.

The door opened with a bang. Several mercenaries looked up in its direction. After noting who entered, the majority returned their attention to what they were doing.

Leonhardt sat in his usual spot at the back of the room with a thud. A boy who helped with routine tasks for the company brought over a filled mug. "Welcome back, boss."

"Thanks," Leonhardt responded shortly and gulped down the mug of water.

You read that right: water. Not alcohol. Sure, based on his looks, one might assume Leonhardt was the type to drink, and sure, he was—but responsibly. It was still early in the day, and Leonhardt never drank when he knew there was a possibility he might have to enter the field.

Despite his rough appearance, Leonhardt treated his job with utmost seriousness.

The boy left Leonhardt, and a tall man came over to replace him. This was Leonhardt's second-in-command. "You're back."

"That I am. Ugh, I hate dealing with nobles."

"Ha ha. So, how'd it go?"

"Not bad, I guess."

The man chuckled as he took the seat across from Leonhardt, and Leonhardt frowned at him with an unamused expression.

"Not bad?" asked the second-in-command. "What's that supposed to mean?"

"Huh? It means what it means. It looks like we're not going to have any problems on our expeditions."

"So, he's not one of those rotten nobles, then."

"Nah. He seemed matter-of-fact, and he didn't put on airs with me. He didn't seem the underhanded type, either."

Leonhardt's second-in-command looked relieved. When they had heard the palace knights were coming, more than anything, Leonhardt and his men had feared the knights would get in the way of their ability to do good work.

While Daniel, the lord of Klausner's Domain, was different, some nobles terminally looked down on commoners. Those same people did whatever they could to stay at the top, never allowing themselves to fall behind common folk. That was the kind of person Leonhardt's second-in-command referred to when he said "rotten noble."

As a matter of course, the nobility tended to lead the knightly Orders. If the knight commander of the Third Order was that sort of person, Leonhardt and his men knew there was a possibility the knights would try to interfere with the mercenaries' expeditions in order to highlight their own achievements.

In these days, when the monster threat had grown so great, the mercenaries recognized their ability to deal with that threat was growing more limited, and theoretically, they welcomed help. But they wouldn't tolerate losing anyone just because some high and mighty lord had to get his way. That went well beyond the scope of what they were willing to put up with.

As such, although Knight Commander Hawke had left a good impression, it was too early to trust him. Most nobles were good at keeping up appearances. If the knight commander was also this regrettable type, there was no telling what the man was actually thinking.

However, Leonhardt trusted his intuition. Perhaps you could call it a sixth sense, but he was a pretty good judge of character. The mercenaries knew this about him from experience. And here Leonhardt was, saying his meeting with Albert hadn't been that bad. His second-in-command hoped that meant the knights wouldn't ultimately give them cause for concern.

"Hmm. Well, so long as they don't try to get in our way," he said.

"For that, we'll just have to wait and see. Also...it looks like the Saint is going to be joining the expedition as well."

"Wait, you mean to tell me that rumor was true?"

"Seems so. The knight commander said himself that she went with 'em."

Word was that the Saint had joined the knights on an expedition into the forests surrounding the capital. Word also was that after she'd gone with them, the capital had experienced a drastic decrease in its monster population.

But "word" came from merchants as they traveled from town to town, and these words had a way of getting embellished with each retelling. Also, there were just as many rumors saying that the Saint actually spent all her time cooped up in the palace and had never so much as glimpsed an expedition.

As such, Leonhardt and his men only half-believed the rumor about the Saint actually joining one. If anything, they could buy that she'd maybe passed by the expedition while it was still outside the famously treacherous Ghoshe Forest.

However, according to the knight commander, those rumors were entirely true.

"At any rate, the Third Order is going to cover the forest. We'll be fighting outside of it. They're not going to get in our way," Leonhardt said.

"That so? Here's hoping they don't bungle it and wind up pushing all the monsters out into the fields."

"They're going to start with preliminary surveys, so I don't think we have to worry about that—much."

"Huh, you seem surprisingly confident in them. Is this your intuition at work?"

"Yeah... Yeah, that man knows what he's doing."

"Heh. Well, if you say so, then it must be true." Leonhardt's second-in-command gave a wry smile, though he still thought they needed to prepare for what was to come.

Leonhardt's intuition was usually right, but just in case... It was best to be prepared for any eventuality.

The two of them kept this wariness in mind as they began to discuss their new plans.

One spring afternoon, soft rays illuminated a quiet room, within which Johan penned a certain document. He finished the page he was working on, laid down his pen, and rubbed his shoulder with an audible pop.

He glanced at the door, but it didn't seem like anyone would be coming in. He looked then to his nearby cup and found it empty. He sighed and picked up the cup as he stood. Then he headed to the kitchen that had been added in the institute during the past year.

"May I help you, Lord Valdec?" the chef asked when she saw him come in.

"Could I get some tea?"

"Right away." The chef took the cup and headed off.

Johan watched absentmindedly, since all he could do now was wait for her to finish preparing his tea.

It hadn't been that long since the kitchen had been built, and it had become normal to have hot water already prepared. The chefs had begun doing so, as Sei drank a great deal of tea while she worked. It didn't take that much extra work for them to keep hot water on hand, as they were always boiling water while making lunch and dinner.

Now that this hot water was regularly available, other researchers had taken up drinking tea as well. As it turned out, Johan was one of them.

Sure, some people had drunk tea before the kitchen—though how was it they'd made hot water again? Ah, right. They had used their research apparatuses. Huh.

Everyone's new tea habit wasn't the only thing that had changed with the new kitchen. Before the dining hall, a number of the researchers had fallen out of the habit of eating anything that resembled actual food—perhaps because the palace dining hall was so far away. But since the kitchen, and since Sei's cooking, even those researchers had started eating proper meals.

The shortened distance was one thing, but the meals themselves were divine, so much so that even Johan, who never had much of an interest in food before, found himself snitching bites in the name of taste-testing whenever Sei was in the kitchen.

Honestly, since her arrival, the atmosphere of the institute had changed quite a bit.

"Johan?"

Johan heard a voice from behind him and turned to find Jude arriving with a cup in hand, just like Johan had done.

"Did you come here for tea, too?" Jude asked.

"You caught me," said Johan. "You, too?"

"Yup. Sei usually makes tea around this time, so I wound up getting into the habit."

"Is that so?"

"She did that to you too, though, didn't she? Since she'd always make you a cup."

Johan touched his chin as he thought. Sei had indeed been in the habit of bringing tea to his office. "Huh, you're right."

Just a few minutes ago, I did feel like something was missing... Was this it? I didn't even notice how much she'd changed me. Johan couldn't help but smile a bit tightly.

Jude wore a curious expression as he noticed Johan's odd look.

"I wonder what she's up to right about now," Johan suddenly wondered out loud.

"Hmm. Probably doing what she always does."

"Indeed, considering where she's gone. I'm sure she's making potions already."

"And probably too many."

The two of them imagined Sei's antics in faraway Klausner's Domain. Sure in their belief that she would be the same old Sei, the two shared a chuckle. Klausner's Domain was known as the alchemist's holy land. If anything, she was probably more energized than usual.

"I bet she's probably cooking, too," Jude said.

"Oh, I don't know about that. I did warn her not to cook in public places."

"Oh, yeah, I remember. But she is with the Third Order, right?"

Johan wore a look that made Jude worry he'd triggered some unpleasant memory.

Sei was earnest to her core, and she obeyed Johan's directions without question. When they'd found out that Sei's cooking considerably improved the physical abilities of those who consumed it, she had conscientiously obeyed his command not to cook in public. However, she still cooked in private—like in the institute's kitchen, for example.

As such, the majority of Sei's cooking filled the bellies of the researchers, but she had once shared it with the Third Order, as they had heard how delicious her cooking was and had specifically asked for it. The Third Order had also been there when they discovered the effects of Sei's cooking, so as there was no point trying to hide her skills from them, Johan had permitted her to cook for them.

Naturally, he had made sure the knights kept the effects of her cooking a closely guarded secret. That had been the condition for allowing them to continue to consume her food. However, since she had received permission once, there was a chance Sei would cook for the knights again if they asked her and were the only ones around, no matter the location.

Johan knew Sei indulged those close to her and was the type of person who hated turning down requests. In fact, even if the knights didn't ask her to cook for them, chances were she would end up doing it anyway while she made food for herself. She had done the same at the institute, after all.

Johan looked up, contemplative. He had been instructed by the palace to keep Sei's extraordinary powers secret, especially those that went beyond the scope of the stories told of the Saint. Some of the abilities she displayed were unbelievable. Just what kind of chaos would ensue if they got out?

Johan understood why the palace was so concerned, and why they had ordered such secrecy, and he had carried out their wishes to the best of his own ability.

However, of all Sei's powers, her cooking prowess was relatively reasonable. The food she made didn't have as much of an effect as her potions, so really, Johan probably didn't need to worry about it in the same way. At any rate, Sei wasn't the only person who could make meals that improved physical abilities. So long as a person possessed skills in Cooking, they could make beneficial dishes as well, although there was, as ever, a difference in the degree of effectiveness.

Not to mention, there isn't anything I can do now that

she's off in a faraway place, Johan thought. For the time being, he had to leave Sei in his best friend's care. He told himself to stop getting so hung up on it.

"I think I'm getting hungry," Johan said. Thinking about Sei's cooking was starting to rouse his appetite.

"Oh, I was just thinking the same thing."

The two of them chuckled dryly together. Sei sure had changed them.

Just then, the chef walked over with a tray in hand. "Sorry to have kept you waiting."

"Huh? What's this?"

"I thought the two of you might be getting hungry."

On top of the tray were two big plates with a cup filled with herbal tea on each. Accompanying the cups were two types of sandwiches that Sei had once made. One had finely chopped cucumbers and herbs with mayonnaise while the other was a boiled egg sandwich.

The chef had remembered what Sei often made for afternoon tea. Anyone's stomach would grumble a little upon seeing such scrumptious fare.

"Thanks," Johan said to the chef. "Nice timing."

"Thank you," Jude echoed. "Well, Johan, I should get back to my desk."

"As should I." Johan cleared his throat and took a plate from the tray.

Jude followed suit and turned on his heel to head back toward the workroom. While Jude left, Johan looked down at the plate. It was quite large, which was far from customary in the Kingdom of Salutania, which tended toward tiny plates for any sort of meal—but the larger one was much easier to carry. Sei often chose such plates so she could carry her meal and snacks together.

Johan and Jude were far from the only ones who'd been changed by Sei. She had a way of affecting everyone in her orbit even while she claimed she wanted to live a normal life. She would no doubt be guilty of wreaking the same sort of changes in Klausner's Domain as well.

It was all too easy to imagine Albert staggering to keep up with her whirlwind.

As Johan walked down the hallway, he surreptitiously chuckled to himself, imagining what troubles awaited his friend. Dish in one hand, he returned to his office, hoping things went for the best with the two of them.

The Saint's
Magic Power is
Omnipotent

ACT
4

Ingredients

JUST AS I WAS GETTING used to daily life in Klausner's Domain, I started feeling the itch to cook a new dish—the food on offer here was great, don't get me wrong, but, well...

Lord Klausner and the castle chefs took great care with our meals. Breakfast was the same as what was typically served across the Kingdom of Salutania, but for other meals, they painstakingly prepared dishes they heard were popular in the palace. In other words, we were eating practically the same food every day.

I understood this as a gesture in the name of making me feel comfortable, and for that I was grateful. However, the teeny tiny repertoire was starting to feel really, you know, small.

In this world, where means of communication were limited, the amount of information circulated to the countryside was limited as well. The only thing the chefs out here really knew about the dishes popular in the palace was that herbs were used when roasting meat or making soups.

Going off that scant information, they regularly incorporated herbs into their cooking—and in greater quantity than I had originally used, which made their dishes especially flavorful.

However, they stuck to roasts and soups. They could have added herbs to pan-fried cuts or grilled fish, but for some reason they didn't. Maybe they were afraid of messing up? I could only guess. In any case, the result was a seemingly endless train of soup, roast, soup, roast, soup, roast, etc.

The chefs were so good at using herbs on the dishes they did make that I was sure they'd do wonderfully with new types, but I would have felt terrible complaining about the food they worked so hard to make. Also, it would have been rude as heck.

But sometimes I just craved a sandwich, or maybe some fish. Before long, I began fantasizing about an expanded Klausner recipe book.

Back at the institute, I would have just made something new myself without a second thought, but my options were limited here. In order to cook, I needed somewhere to do the cooking.

If I wanted to use the castle kitchens, naturally I would need Lord Klausner's permission. And though I had experience cooking outdoors, it took a bit more preparation than kitchen work.

Not to mention, it would be one thing to cook over an open fire on an expedition, but if I were to do so somewhere near the castle grounds, I would definitely garner troublesome attention. Also, Lord Klausner would doubtless make assumptions, like that I was displeased by food he served. I would feel awful if he thought that, especially since he and his staff were going so far to cater to my tastes.

Was there somewhere I could cook in secret?

"Hmm..."

"What's the matter?" asked one of the knights, concerned by the crease in my brow.

I was in the knights' quarters, and I had sunk into thought as I waited for the assistant to count the potions I had delivered.

"Oh, nothing, just something that's been on my mind." I felt like I could confide in him since he was part of the Third Order, but I was afraid of anything I said accidentally reaching Lord Klausner in a negative light.

How can I put it? As I struggled to answer, another knight came over to check on me as well.

"What's going on? If there's anything bothering you, feel free to tell us."

"It's no big deal," I assured him.

"It's fine if you don't want to talk about it, but sometimes it's better to get things off your chest."

"Really, it's nothing. I was just thinking about how I'd like to cook again—it might be a nice change of pace."

"You're going to cook?!" the knight exclaimed as his eyes lit up.

Other knights heard as well, and they all started gathering around, asking what I was planning to make. Some even had direct requests that they actively discussed with each other.

How did this happen? I liked making potions, and it wasn't like I was tired of that, but fatigue with your routine is totally normal. I'd thought defaulting to the change of pace excuse would work, but I hadn't expected this level of enthusiasm.

When I asked, tentatively, I learned the meals the knights ate out here weren't the same as the ones I got in the castle. Lord Hawke and I were given seasoned dishes, but the knights were making do with typical Salutanian fare. Seasoned dishes were more expensive, so it couldn't be helped. Also, the castle chefs had figured the knights were used to unseasoned dishes, so they hadn't thought anyone would be disappointed.

However, the knights knew what they were missing. I had cooked for them on expeditions, after all. Plus, so long as they paid, people from outside the institute were allowed to eat at our dining hall—though the knights didn't always have the time to come.

In any case, since coming to Klausner's Domain, they'd been thoroughly deprived of even the option of better fare. They had resolved themselves to grin and bear it since they were here on the job, but now they were excited.

"What's all this commotion about?"

"Oh, Knight Commander."

Knight Commander Albert Hawke descended from the second floor, frowning at the ruckus.

When I told Albert what I'd said, he nodded in understanding and gave me a somewhat tight smile. "I see now."

"But I don't have anywhere to cook, so it's not like I could in the first place. I doubt they'd let me borrow the castle kitchens. Maybe I could do something in the brewery?"

"Would that be possible?"

"They've got cauldrons and stuff, so if I tried, probably. But I have a feeling I'd get yelled at."

The brewery had a hearth and a ton of pots and so forth, which were, granted, usually used for potions. However, everyone there *lived* for potions. I couldn't imagine how irritated they'd be if I defiled the tools of their trade for the sake of my hobby. And I doubted Corinna would give me permission in the first place.

"We have a small kitchen here," said Albert. "You could use that if you'd like, but..."

"You don't have anything I could use for boiling water?"

"Unfortunately, no. Every time we want to make tea, we have to send the chamberlain to the castle kitchens."

"I see."

I could probably whip *something* up if I used the small kitchen in the knights' quarters, like Albert had suggested. However, even if I could make enough for a few people, I wouldn't be able to feed the whole Order.

If I wanted access to a bigger kitchen, then the only option besides the one in the castle was probably this one dining hall I knew of in town. However, I didn't know anyone there. And there was no way they would consent to letting me, a stranger, and the Saint no less, use their kitchens. Alas.

It wasn't like I wanted to cook so badly that I'd ask people I didn't know to let me take over their kitchen.

"You'll be able to do some cooking when we head out

on the expedition," said Albert. "You'll just have to hang on until then."

"Yeah... That's too bad."

"Are you all right?"

"I don't want to make a big deal out of it or anything, I'm just a bit tired of the castle menu. They're probably not going to change it up any time soon, right?"

Albert paused, then leaned forward and brought his lips to my ear to whisper: "I understand completely."

I looked up at him as he drew back with a slightly awkward, shy look on his face. I gave an equally awkward smile back.

No matter how much we liked roasts, it didn't mean we wanted to eat them prepared the same way every day, even if they did alternate between meats, cuts, and herbs.

"I wish they would at least add fish to the menu," I said.

"I know what you mean, but we'd have to request it specifically first."

"It's so hard to ask for anything," I moaned.

Although I now knew Albert shared my opinion, I was still at square one for places where I could actually do anything about our monotonous meal misery. In the end, we agreed that we'd both be counting the days until the expedition.

Having finished my potion delivery in the morning, in the afternoon, Corinna and I headed to the herb fields. When we were done with our lesson there, I was free for the rest of the day.

On the road back from the fields, we passed a market just inside the gates on the way to the castle. It wasn't as big as the one in the capital, but they sold a variety of things, so I liked window shopping.

It had been a year since my summoning, but I could count on one hand how many times I had been to the markets in the capital, so that probably made this experience all that much more exciting for me.

Considering the conversation I'd had with the knights about cooking that morning, I found myself perusing ingredients.

As I looked around, Corinna chuckled. "There you go again. It's not like there's anything all that unusual here."

"But you never know, there might be."

"Maybe something unfamiliar to you, but I come here practically every day. I know everything on display."

Corinna had a point. The market was where everyone in the domain bought their food, after all. However, as I searched, I came across ingredients I'd never seen in the capital—both those unique to this world and ingredients I recognized from back in Japan. I wasn't about to dismiss this remarkable spread.

"That reminds me, didn't you say something about knowing how to cook?" Corinna mused.

"You got me. I used to cook a bit back in the capital."

"You're an odd one. I didn't believe it the first time I heard. Not at all."

I smiled stiffly. Corinna had been duly shocked when I mentioned my cooking one day. It made sense, though. People of high station in Salutania rarely knew a pot from a pan, let alone how to use either, and as much as I hated admitting it, the Saint was pretty darn high up on the social ladder. However, when I explained to Corinna that I was a commoner by origin, it all seemed to make more sense to her.

"So you used to cook back where you came from?"

"Yup. However, it's not like I can get all the ingredients I'm familiar with, so my actual repertoire is kinda limited."

The dishes I made back in the capital were, broadly speaking, what I would call a taste of home. But that wasn't the case, not really. Ever since I got to this world, I had mostly been making Western recipes, not Japanese ones.

Did I miss Japanese food such as rice and miso soup? Of course. I would have made them ages ago if I could have. Why hadn't I? Duh: I couldn't get the proper ingredients.

I kept thinking I might find them if I only looked hard enough, but I had yet to find *any* of what I considered the absolute basics—you know, miso, soy sauce, or the dried seaweed and fish flakes that made Japanese soup stock. I understood that, theoretically, I could make miso on my own, but I had never done it before, so I had no idea how.

It would have been nice if I could find it somewhere in this world, but I feared I might have to reconcile with the idea of going the rest of my life without ever tasting it again.

Auuugh, thinking that made me want to eat it all the more! *I better stop, or this is going to become a straight-up deadly craving.*

"You mean there are some things you can't make? Like those medicinal dishes you were talking about before?"

"Yeah, part of it is that I can't get the ingredients, but for those in particular I also just don't know how."

"Oh, is that so?"

"Yeah. I know what they are conceptually, but I don't know the proper techniques or anything."

"That's too bad."

Corinna and the other alchemists were still taken with the idea of this medicinal cuisine. My vague, piecemeal knowledge made it really hard to answer any of their questions, so much so that I'd often sit there in a bit of a daze, combing through my brain for any useful tidbit.

I should stop trying to tell people about things I know nothing about. Next time I'll just apologize and say I'm not going to be very useful. Yeah, that's the ticket. I pulled myself together and moved on to the next storefront, where they dealt largely in grains.

They displayed their wares in piles of stacked burlap bags filled with various types of grains. The staple starch in the Kingdom of Salutania was bread, so most of the bags were filled with wheat—and not just one type, either, but different varieties. Back in Japan, I had only ever seen refined, processed grains, but these were still whole.

As I studied them, admiring how many kinds there were, I heard the shopkeeper telling a customer, "This one's got a hard husk."

A hard husk? I unconsciously came to a stop upon hearing that.

"What is it?" Corinna asked.

"Sorry, I found something I'd like to examine."

"Which one?"

"That wheat." I pointed at the kind the shopkeeper was showing his customer.

Corinna recognized it and told me it was called spelt, which was the same name as a kind of wheat that had been cultivated long ago in Europe.

"It's used pretty commonly around here. Why did it pique your interest?"

"I read about it in a book back home."

According to that book, I explained, spelt had a cosmic ton of nutrients compared to more common wheat varieties. A woman in the book, one who had been canonized as a saint back in Europe, had declared it to be the best kind of wheat.

I had never seen spelt in person, but I'd known it was renowned for its hard husk, which was why the shopkeeper's words had caught my ear.

As I told Corinna about this book, she raised an eyebrow. The part about "nutrients" had aroused her interest. Apparently, they didn't yet have a concept of nutrients in this world.

As a result, I wound up rambling about how a balanced diet leads to a healthy body and stuff like that. I didn't know that much about the topic, so I could only describe things in broad, general terms. I also explained that proper nutrients could help you fend off illness or even cure some ailments. I knew this idea wasn't unique to Japan and was rather a concept adopted from Chinese practice.

Ideas get adopted and adapted all the time. My teacher in the aromatherapy class I'd taken during my spare time had once said something about how the basis of all health comes down to diet. And I was pretty sure she had mentioned that proper meals were the foundation of that.

The West had developed a similar philosophy in its monasteries long ago. The type of research they had conducted there had focused on herbs and cooking. I had read in a book that they had used herbs both for their seasoning and their medicinal benefits.

"And to think I've eaten spelt without a second thought all this time. Our wheat's tremendously valuable, then," Corinna said.

"That's how I see it."

"I wonder what kind of potions we could make with it...?"

"Huh? You can make a potion out of wheat?"

Wait—I'd been thinking about using spelt for food, not potions.

The book I'd read had included recipes by the European saint. As I tried to recall those recipes, I realized the rest of the ingredients were all things I could find in Klausner's Domain. *I bet I could recreate them. Maybe I should give it a try.*

"I could definitely make something to eat with it, at least," I said.

"With spelt, you mean?"

"Exactly," I said, and I described some of the recipes I was thinking of.

If a person with Cooking skills made food, they could improve the physical abilities of those who ate their cooking. Even food made with regular ingredients could have a noticeable impact on the person who ate it. I couldn't help but wonder what would happen if I made a meal using something as nutritionally potent as spelt.

If I could recreate those recipes, then I bet I could do some fantastic things for the castle menu. This could be my chance.

"It's not *quite* like the medicinal cuisine I mentioned before, but I just might be able to make something with similar effects," I said.

"Is that so?"

"I'd like to give it a try, if I may. Do you think I could borrow the castle kitchens?"

Corinna's eyes glinted at the mention of the medicinal food. Whatever I made wouldn't be that exactly, but it would doubtless turn out healthy.

Corinna must have been pretty interested to see what I might whip up, judging from the great big smile she had on her face when she said she'd make a special request to Lord Klausner—one that would allow me to use the kitchens.

Two days after I told Corinna about spelt, I entered the brewery, and Corinna announced that I had received permission to use the kitchens. She had made haste in getting permission from Lord Klausner, which he'd given readily upon hearing Corinna's explanation.

He even said he was looking forward to eating the kinds of dishes that were so popular in the capital. The castle chefs had a similar take and were delighted to get a chance to learn directly from me.

I felt a bit bad, though, since what I was thinking of making wasn't remotely fancy.

Preparations were made in the blink of an eye, and soon the day came when I at last entered the castle kitchens. When Corinna and I arrived, we were greeted by a whole bevy of smiling chefs.

"Thank you for allowing us this opportunity to learn the most avant-garde recipes from the capital," one chef said to me.

"No, no, please, I should be thanking you for granting my sudden request. I look forward to cooking with you today."

"It will be our pleasure," they all said together.

I was surprised enough by their gratitude—really, I was the grateful one here!—but I wasn't planning on making something I had made in the capital, so I hoped I could meet their expectations.

After greetings were over, I tied on an apron and set about cooking. The countertop was already covered with the ingredients I had asked to be prepared ahead of time.

Today, I was going to be making pasta.

First, I mixed the wheat flour made from spelt together with oil, egg, and salt. Unfortunately, they didn't have olive oil, so I had to use a different kind of vegetable oil.

A long time ago, I had wanted to try making pasta by hand, but I never ended up doing so, so I had a pretty shoddy recollection of how exactly it was made. I warned the chefs that I was just going to be experimenting for the most part, so hopefully they would forgive me if I royally messed it up.

Yeah, okay, backup plan—if this goes weird, I'll just ask permission to try something else, I thought.

Once I showed them this first part, the other chefs set about making pasta with me. To tell you the truth, they were part of my experiment as well. I wanted to find out if using spelt made a difference versus other kinds of wheat. Therefore, we had to prepare two kinds of pasta: one made from spelt and the other made from another variety.

Also, when word got out that I was going to cook, an unexpected number of people said they wanted to try whatever I made. First there was Lord Klausner and Corinna, then there were the other members of Lord Klausner's family and the alchemists in the brewery. I could never have made enough pasta for that many people on my own, so I was getting help.

I wanted the chefs' help for another reason, too: my fifty-percent-bonus curse.

Because I had the Cooking skill, the food I made increased a person's abilities, and it was also fifty percent more effective than food made by someone with an equivalent skill level. This was why Johan had forbidden me from cooking in public spaces. However, he hadn't forbidden me from ever cooking at all. In fact, I cooked all the time at the institute.

I think he'd put the kibosh on it because it'd be a problem if too many people knew about my ability. I understood, so my portions would be going to Albert and Lord Klausner's family. This was a small number of people, and other than Albert, none of them did much strenuous activity, so I didn't think they would notice the difference in effects.

I also wanted them to have my cooking because, well, I was the one making it. I mean, doesn't the idea of a meal made by the Saint herself have a special ring to it? *Although it does feel kinda awkward to consider my own food as special... But people in high positions like that sort of thing, so...*

I had asked Albert, and he'd said it sounded like a good idea.

At any rate, I was impressed by the skill on display as the chefs kneaded the pasta dough. They'd only just listened to my explanation, and here they were, masters in the making. Incredible.

For myself, I was lagging behind. *I better focus up and stop getting distracted.*

When the surface of the dough became smooth, I put a wet cloth over it and set it aside. Then I started working on the vegetables I was going to add into the dish.

Meat sauce would've been delicious, but since I wanted to feature herbs, I decided to make basil pasta. I had a vague feeling that there had been mainly herb-flavored pastas in that book I had read.

I chopped up garlic, onion, basil, and dill. Tragically, the onion made my eyes water like crazy.

Just as I was finished, it was time to start working on the pasta again. I stretched the dough until it was thin, folded it into layers, and then chopped it up to make flat noodles.

Normally, I preferred pasta that was much thinner, but this was the extent of what I could make with my own two hands. They probably weren't the right kind of noodles for basil pasta, either, but I had given up.

Next, I had to boil the pasta, cook the noodles with the vegetables, and add the seasoning. Then it would be done.

"How's it going?" Corinna asked as I hovered over the boiling pot.

"It'll be ready soon."

She peered into the pot with a great deal of interest from her spot beside me. It was a big pot, so seeing that tiny woman leaning over it brought a smile to my face.

"You called this 'pasta,' right? What was the point of changing the type of wheat?"

"I want to see if it makes a difference in the overall effects."

"The effects?"

"Yeah, you know, like how Cooking skills impact food, which in turn impacts physical abilities."

"Eh? That's the first time I've ever heard of that."

"Oh, I thought I mentioned it—it's been the talk of the capital this year. I guess word hadn't reached you guys yet."

"Maybe so. Or perhaps my old ears weren't paying attention to anything unrelated to potions. That's quite interesting, though."

It really did take forever for information to travel in this world and its total lack of telephones or television.

This may sound unbelievable, but my grandma once said that when she was young, it took years for the latest trends in the capital to reach the countryside. And that was when they already had both phones and TV! If what my grandma said was true, then I could absolutely understand why Klausner's Domain was out of the loop on what was considered common knowledge in the capital.

While we talked, the pasta finished boiling, so I drained the water and tossed the noodles into the frying pan I had at the ready.

I started off with a single portion. I was planning to have the chefs taste it, after which they would make their own portions.

The head chef stood opposite Corinna to watch what I did. The other chefs studied me from a short distance away, so I couldn't help but feel nervous from my skin to my bones.

I only added salt to make the flavor pop, but when I tasted the pasta after—it was delicious. Bright, fresh, and just a little rich. I plated the noodles and stepped back.

"It's done," I declared as I placed the plate in front of the head chef. She quickly reached to take a taste.

As she did, her eyes widened, her mouth went slack, and then—she smiled in utter delight. That look really made a weight fall right off my shoulders.

"This is herb-flavored pasta handmade by Lady Sei," the butler announced as all the plates were brought out at once.

It was finally time for everyone to get a taste.

In the dining hall, I sat with Lord Klausner, his family, and Albert.

"I have very much been looking forward to trying your cooking," Lord Klausner's wife told me excitedly.

"I hope you enjoy it," I responded with an awkward chuckle. *Please let the flavor be okay.*

Though the butler had said I'd made it, really, it was the head chef who had put it all together. All I'd done was make the pasta. I felt a bit conflicted being given the credit for the important parts—you know, like the seasoning? Oh well.

I'd had no choice but to ask the head chef to finish preparing the dishes so that I could be seated at the table with Lord Klausner and everyone else. I didn't even have the option to enjoy eating on my own later—I had suggested this, but the butler vetoed it.

"Please eat before it grows cold."

Simultaneously, everyone took their first bite. As soon as I did, a refreshing flavor spread through my mouth. The fragrance of the herbs accented the flavor, and although besides the herbs it was only seasoned with salt, it was absolutely delectable. *Great job, head chef!*

I heard comments all through the dining hall about how amazing the dish smelled and how mouthwateringly good it was, too. As I scanned the room, everyone had smiles on their faces. I was relieved to see the noble family was enjoying their meal.

"So this is what you call 'pasta'? I heard that you made this with flour," Lord Klausner said.

"That's right."

"I also heard this was a recipe from the country you came from, but, you know, I've actually eaten something similar to this before."

"You have?"

"Not in the kingdom, but once, when I went abroad. It was a dish eaten quite frequently by commoners as well. I believe they called it 'noodles.'"

"Noodles! Maybe it's the same type of food as pasta after all. They're synonyms, in a way."

"Oh, is that so?"

He told me more about this foreign dish he'd tried, which had involved pouring a sauce over noodles. I hadn't seen a single noodle dish since my summoning, so I had assumed they simply didn't exist in Salutania. However, it turned out that, while not common in this kingdom, noodles did exist in other countries in this world. Maybe it had to do with the availability of ingredients?

I'll ask the merchant who stops by the institute later, I thought.

Then I heard a surprised "Hm?" from right next to me.

I looked toward the sound to find Albert furrowing his brow.

"Is something the matter?" I asked.

"No, nothing..." he trailed off, seeming somewhat evasive.

I wonder what it could be? Albert had said he wasn't picky about his food, but herbs were still pretty new for every Salutanian palate. Could it be he didn't like one of the kinds I'd used today? *No...but I've used all these herbs at the institute before. It can't be that. Then what is it?*

I peered closely at Albert's face, but he just gave me a forced yet perplexed smile and deflected with a, "Never mind."

At the same time, I felt like I heard someone nearby gasp, but that was probably just my imagination.

The dinner party came to a successful end, and before I knew it, it was the following day. When I went to deliver potions to the knights in their quarters, I finally learned why Albert had made that face.

"It recovered your HP?" I echoed, eyes wide.

"Yeah, that's right. Only some of us got that effect, though."

Ultimately, I'd given in and done some more vigorous experiments with my pasta—some had gone to the Knights of the Third Order. I just really wanted to know about the effects, okay?

And anyway, I'd had the knights participate in my cooking research before, so they were used to it. And they immediately agreed to participating this time, since it meant they got to eat something different *and* delicious.

As it turned out, the two pasta types had produced clearly different results. In addition to the empowering effects of pasta made from regular wheat, pasta made from spelt also recovered missing HP.

I'd been extremely careful about keeping my ingredients and methodology exactly the same in every respect for both batches, so it was probably safe to assume that HP recovery was an effect of spelt.

Albert had no doubt been experiencing this effect when he made that face at the dinner table.

"When you say it recovered your HP, do you mean you were instantly healed?" I asked the knight.

"No, it was a gradual recovery over time."

I asked because I was now wondering if this spelt pasta could be used in place of a potion, but this gradual recovery was certainly different. The knights had also found that today, they'd needed less time to recover between training sessions.

A knight who had been listening to our conversation piped up. "I'm pretty sure it increased the rate at which we naturally recover HP, too."

"Oh, that could be what's going on," one of the knights said thoughtfully.

"Oh, has your interval shortened?" I asked.

"More or less. I *think* I'm getting back more over the same period of time. I'd have to check, though."

To be sure, they would've had to check their stats after eating the meal, then checked again after a set interval and compared their recovery to what it was on a day when they hadn't eaten the spelt pasta. As they talked this over, the knights started glancing at me with mournful eyes.

Demanding seconds, eh? Fine, fine.

I would have to borrow the kitchens again to figure this out. The only problem would be whether I could get permission a second time.

"I'll see if I can get back into the kitchens," I told them with a tentative smile.

"Oh, right. This isn't the palace."

"Too bad."

The knights resigned themselves as well.

It seemed like the herb-flavored pasta really had been a surprisingly big hit. The knights seemed more disappointed that they wouldn't get the chance to eat it again than by the fact that we wouldn't be able to research its effects.

While we were discussing this, Albert came downstairs. "I didn't know you were here, Sei."

"Oh, I came to deliver some potions again."

"Thanks. We'll need those." At Albert's direction, one of the knights picked the box of potions up from the table and carried it into the back.

Ah, right. I had completely forgotten why I was here and wound up getting absorbed in talking in the hall.

I was here for *two* reasons, actually. The first was to deliver the potions. The other was to ask Albert if there had been any recent developments in the surveys. I had been planning to ask about the food after I completed those first two objectives, but the knights caught me when I was passing them on my way to Albert's office. I should have stopped myself and gone straight to Albert. I had told him that I was coming today, after all.

"I'm sorry, I was planning to go directly to you, but they were talking about last night's dinner, and before I knew it..."

"Ah, yes. That was utterly divine." That dazzling smile of his spread across his face.

I'd thought I was used to it by now, but it was still hard to keep looking at Albert when he did that. I desperately tried to switch gears and focus on the conversation. "Th-thank you. The knights were just telling me their thoughts."

"Were they now? They've been talking about it all morning."

"Speaking of which—I was wondering if you made that face because you noticed its effects, too?"

"Ha, so I did. I wasn't sure it was quite the moment to discuss it, so I held back at the time."

Albert had kept quiet so as not to draw the attention of Lord Klausner and his family. Although the effects of my cooking had become common knowledge in the palace, it was often hard to tell just how much information had been released to the public, so he'd avoided making an observation just in case.

From there, we really dug into the effects of spelt. Because the knights had been talking about it since that morning, Albert had quite a few reports to pass on.

"I suppose we can't say if it has healing effects in itself or if it actually increases the speed of our bodily processes. I'd have to make more batches to really investigate this," I said.

"That could be difficult. The chefs have a job to do in there, too."

"Yeah... I guess it'd be better to wait until we get back to the palace, then."

"So long as we know it hastens HP recovery, that's good enough for me. We can discern the underlying mechanics later."

After all, being able to recover HP more quickly during the expedition might well become critical—someone's life could end up depending on it.

But, well, it would be hard to traipse around the forest armed with pasta. I doubted it would stay good if they brought it in a lunchbox or something. However, if the HP recovery effect was a particular characteristic of spelt, maybe I could figure out a way to make something more practically useful out of it.

I sure wish I could experiment with spelt bread or something... I guess I'll have to wait until we get back to the palace, I thought as I left the knights' quarters.

The Saint's*
*Magic Power is *
Omnipotent

ACT
5

The Saint's Magic

"I NEVER IMAGINED simple wheat would have such an effect," Corinna said with admiration as she gazed at the spelt specimen on her desk.

The day after I made pasta, when I got to the brewery, everyone immediately swarmed around me. They had already heard about my discoveries from Corinna.

The alchemists in the brewery had a vested interest in herbs, so I had predicted this. However, at the time, I still hadn't heard the additional news from the Third Order, so the group broke up quickly.

Of course, that wasn't the end of it. When I got back from dropping off the potions for the knights, they gathered around me once more with new questions. I ended up telling them everything I'd investigated up to that point.

"So you see, among all the wheat varieties, spelt is known for its high nutritional value."

"Is this related to that medicinal cooking business?"

"Not exactly, but it's similar enough."

I had stumbled on that book about the European saint and her spelt fixation while browsing the aromatherapy shelf at a bookstore. That saint had studied medicine and herbology and made great achievements in food research, which was how she'd come to be known for evangelizing spelt—she'd even written a book on it.

"Now *that's* interesting," one of the alchemists said. "Are there any other kinds of food like this?"

"A ton. It'd take me ages to tell you about every one of them."

"Let's start from the beginning and go bit by bit, then. First, spelt."

While I did know about those super-hyped ingredients called superfoods and the like, I started to realize I maybe didn't remember all that much about them.

A cold sweat trickled down my back, but thankfully I could handle another mini lecture on spelt, at least.

Corinna picked up the specimen and started muttering to herself as she thought something over. She'd asked about making potions from wheat, right? What kind of things might we concoct? Wheat... Liquid... Beer? Beer was made out of barley, though.

"Do you think that, using spelt, we could make something more effective than high-grade HP potions?" I asked her.

"Oho, is that something you've been looking into?"

"Yes. I've done a great deal of research, but I have yet to find such a potent recipe."

Part of me wondered if it could be so simple as adding spelt to my high-grade HP potion recipe—like some kind of secret recipe of my own. I also still nursed a faint hope that Corinna might have some special folk knowledge on the topic.

My question had been offhanded, and so I was shocked by her answer: "Such a thing did once exist."

"What?! Really?"

"Yes, but not anymore."

Not anymore?! My eyes widened.

I glanced around the room. No one else seemed floored—did they already know about this? Corinna ushered me into the back room, where she unlocked the door to a closed bookcase and retrieved a book. When she flipped through the pages, I realized it contained dozens upon dozens of potion recipes.

"Take a look. This is the recipe you're searching for. Superior-grade, they called it."

"Oh, my..."

"Its effects are remarkable, but it also costs a great deal. The particular herb required to brew it is difficult to acquire and commands a fearsome price at market. On top of that, hardly anyone could ever actually make this recipe, even here in the brewery."

All the alchemists in Klausner's Domain had exceptionally high levels, as one would expect from the place known as the alchemist's holy land. Their Pharmaceuticals skills and techniques were basically from another plane of existence, especially compared to those of the folks back in the capital.

I supposed it was possible I just saw them in a favorable light because Corinna was the head alchemist and all, but they really seemed top-notch. Either way, every potion made here utterly outshone the ones made at the research institute. After all, at the institute, I was the only one who could make high-grade HP potions, but more than a few people here had a high enough level in their Pharmaceuticals skill to do the same.

However, according to Corinna, none possessed the level required to make superior-grade potions. That wasn't for want of natural skill, or a lack of trying—the alchemists here were brilliant, but without the special herb needed to make superior-grade potions, there was no way to do work sufficiently complex enough to raise one's Pharmaceuticals skill to the required level.

The herb in question was found in the far north of Klausner's Domain. It only grew in a select few spots deep within the forest. Despite that, at one time, the people of the domain had managed to cultivate it in their fields, if at the border of the woods.

"Wait, you could grow it? Like, agriculturally?"

"We could indeed."

"But why not now?"

With an odd, nostalgic look, Corinna explained. Once, a truly gifted alchemist had lived in Klausner's Domain. To this day, she was remembered as the mother of modern medicinal know-how, and her influence continued to shape the pharmaceutical industry. The alchemists of Klausner's Domain had revered her and given her the title "Great Alchemist," of which she had clearly been more than worthy.

Notably, all her life she had skirted the border of genius and profound eccentricity. The gossipy types had instead referred to her as the "Fool's Alchemist."

Nevertheless, it was this woman who had made it possible for so many different types of herbs to be cultivated in Klausner's Domain. It seemed to some that she had found a way to cultivate plants that could only be picked in the wild specifically so she could make potions whenever she wanted. She wasn't quoted as saying anything like, "Well, if I can't get the ingredients, then I'll bring the ingredients to me," but that was absolutely the vibe.

The Great Alchemist had also worked on cultivating the special herb for superior-grade potions. However, despite devising a specific technique for its care, growing it was still no mean feat. According to Corinna, it required several very particular conditions for the herb to take.

"Many of those conditions have been kept secret, or even lost," she said. "I can't be certain, but I suspect one of those conditions is no longer being met, which is why we have lost our ability to grow it."

"What do you mean they were kept secret?"

"Only a very few people know every single necessary element for growing the herb." Corinna retrieved another book from the bookcase and handed it to me.

I hesitated to open it, instead looking between the cover of the book and Corinna's face. She jerked her chin to tell me to go ahead, so I started flipping through the pages.

As I read, I furrowed my brow. The contents of this book revealed the very same secret conditions for growing the herb. "Um, are you sure it's okay to show me this?"

"I'm the one in charge here, and I say yes. You don't have a problem with that, do you?"

Really? I had my doubts—this felt too easy—but I looked for the page about the herb in question. Before long, I found it.

As I was reading, Corinna murmured, "This is extremely confidential. Do *not* share what you read here, not with anyone. Although, once you know the conditions, you'll see why nothing can be done."

Sure enough, as I got a bit further, I realized exactly what she meant.

There were bucketloads of information about basic herb cultivation in that book, at least as much as there was about the specific herb for superior-grade potions. It talked about light, water, temperature, fertilizer for keeping the soil in good condition, and all that stuff, but there was one word with which I was unfamiliar, at least in so far as agriculture.

"Blessings?"

I had never, ever in my life seen that word associated with growing plants. It gave me the mental image of someone praying in front of a field. What kind of religious practice would that be?

At the same time, the idea was awfully familiar. My heart skipped a beat.

There's no way. I glanced timidly toward Corinna, who stood next to me, and met her gaze.

"Do you know what this is referring to?" she asked.

"Uh, I'm not exactly sure."

This wasn't a lie, not really. It reminded me of something, sure, but I didn't know anything for certain. Besides, the person who had written this book was the Great Alchemist, not some past Saint. In other words, it was highly likely that the blessing described here wasn't the one I'd been trying to devise. Despite that, I got the feeling that my initial thought wasn't too far off the mark.

"Hm. Too bad, then. Well, never mind." Although Corinna's words were nonchalant, to me, they resonated with a deep disappointment. "Even if we could perform this blessing, no one possesses the requisite skill level to do anything with the herb."

Thoughts whirled round and round in my head. But she was right—no one could make superior-grade HP potions without the necessary skill level.

"That reminds me, I haven't asked you yet, have I?" Corinna peered at me. "What *is* your Pharmaceuticals level anyway?"

I pulled up my Stats to check.

SEI TAKANASHI – Level 56/Saint
HP: 5,003/5,003
MP: 6,173/6,173
BATTLE SKILLS
    Holy Magic: Level ∞
PRODUCTION SKILLS
    Pharmaceuticals: Level 32
    Cooking: Level 15

Huh. Well, it was higher than the last time I had checked. I had assumed I couldn't go up any higher. Maybe I owed this increase to the work I'd done with Corinna's secret recipe? That would be amazing! It'd mean I could continue raising my level even if we never figured out how to grow the special herb again.

"Level 32." I beamed.

Corinna frowned. "What?!"

The intensity of her gaze made me take an involuntary step back. "I-Is something the matter?"

"That level of yours, it's higher than I imagined."

"O-oh?"

"Higher than mine, in fact."

Huh? Really? I gaped.

Her expression melted into exasperation. "Well, I guess it makes sense that someone would reach that level if they could make as many potions as you do every day."

"Uh, sorry." I apologized reflexively.

The alchemists had shown surprise at my production rate, sure, but Corinna hadn't said anything about it, so I hadn't thought much of it. However, it seemed like I got a little potion-happy even by their standards. I'd justified it with the fact that both the knights and the mercenary company were in constant need of a steady supply, but...I probably should have restrained myself a bit.

"At Level 32, you'll have no trouble making superior-grade potions. The only remaining problem is the lack of ingredients."

"I see."

Corinna put a hand to her chin as she sank into thought. I glanced at her sidelong, though my own thoughts were now dominated by superior-grade HP potions.

I wasn't all that surprised to hear that I met the requirements to make them. In fact, I had assumed as much. You see, your ability to make higher grades of potion depended on your skill level, and it increased every ten. I had assumed I would be able to make higher than high-grade potions the minute I hit Level 30, but it turned out the main thing I'd been missing was the correct ingredients.

Those were still a problem. It would be difficult to acquire the missing herb, and certainly I couldn't get it any time soon. We couldn't even think of cultivating it unless we were able to fulfill this "blessing" condition. *Hmm. Should I tell Corinna about what I was trying to do before?*

As I contemplated this, Corinna moved to the double-doored cabinet in the corner of the room. To my surprise, there was a second set of doors behind the first, and these were made of metal. I understood metal cabinets to be rare, and indeed it turned out to be a safe. The key to the safe hung around Corinna's neck. She pulled it out from underneath her clothes.

Inside the safe was a very old-looking book. It was thinner than either the books with the potion recipes or the book about herb cultivation techniques.

What could this one be? I watched cautiously as Corinna held the book out to me.

Tentatively, I opened the cover. While it was in good enough condition, the pages inside were yellowed with age. As I carefully flipped through them, I began to suspect that this book was, in fact, *quite* different from the others.

"Is this a diary?" I asked.

"Yes, but it's an important piece of literature."

Literature? At a cursory skim, it seemed ordinary enough. What could she mean?

"That book is incredibly precious. Please only read it when you're alone in this room."

"Really? Alone?"

"Yes. The contents of that book are highly classified information. They mustn't be shown to anyone else."

Holy crap! What authorized *me* to read top secret intel? Then again, if I asked Corinna, she'd just say something like, "Me, I authorized you."

She prompted me to keep going with her eyes, so I returned my attention to the diary. I placed it on the table and sat so I could really focus on absorbing its contents.

I only had to go a bit further before things started clicking together: the author of this diary was likely the Great Alchemist herself. She had written about her daily life, just like you would in any normal diary, but her daily life included the precise work of trial and error that had led to her incredible feats of cultivation.

"The person who wrote this...don't tell me it was *her*?" I paused to glance at Corinna, who was sitting next to me. She nodded silently.

Yup. It had to be. In this book, the Great Alchemist had also recorded her thought processes, which hadn't been in the book about cultivating herbs. The path to success was never an easy one, but it sounded like she'd enjoyed the ups and downs in equal measure.

However, the diary wasn't all herbs all the time—it also spoke of the Great Alchemist's love for Klausner's Domain and the people who lived here. She was, in fact, the daughter of the Lord Klausner of that era.

It seemed that Klausner's Domain hadn't had a specialty export in those days. It had mainly produced wheat, just like the majority of the other territories in the Kingdom of Salutania.

One year, the wheat harvest was devastatingly poor, and famine spread across the whole of Salutania, including Klausner's Domain. It had hurt the Great Alchemist's heart to see her people starve.

Thus, in order to pay taxes with some kind of crop other than wheat, she had turned to the cultivation of herbs. Of course, her preestablished interest had spurred this decision. However, her words made clear to me that she was driven first and foremost by concern for her people. She was so grateful that her work had ensured they would never again have to fear going hungry.

As I kept turning pages, I found multiple mentions of a certain herb that she was having a hard time cultivating. She was stuck on figuring out its needs—it seemed far trickier to nurse than any other plant. It also seemed to be vitally important; she couldn't just put it aside and come back to it later.

I could feel her frustration in her writing. She recorded failure after failure, and I found myself skimming through all her roadblocks until something caught my eye—a cry of joy. She had at last managed to solve the riddle.

I turned back a few pages, then forward, then back, but there was no mistaking it: a blessing. That was her answer. And there was something else, something I couldn't overlook.

"Golden magic..."

Ah. I knew it.

Corinna studied me as she said, "Do you know what this 'golden magic' refers to?"

Yes. Yes, I did.

For the next few days after I learned the shocking truth, I cooped myself up in the back room of the brewery to read through the Great Alchemist's diary with absolute care, making sure to absorb every word.

I still felt a bit bad about reading someone's diary, but, well, you can't make an omelet without breaking a few eggs. And anyway, I was only doing this because I needed to know how to use my Saintly powers. Or so I told myself.

From the descriptions in the diary, these blessings definitely sounded like the work of the Saint's magic. After all, if the Great Alchemist could use golden magic, she had been the Saint. I had predicted as much.

Corinna confirmed it when I asked her. Unfortunately, they didn't know whether blessings were specifically a power the Saint possessed, as that was confidential information held by the palace. Furthermore, the only people who knew any details about the Great Alchemist's blessings were the generations of lords of Klausner's Domain and the people in charge of the castle brewery. This was also the reason why the diary was kept in absolute secrecy.

I was worried Lord Klausner might object to my reading it, but it turned out to be a baseless fear. Corinna assured me that she had sought his permission ahead of time, and I was relieved to hear it. When I actually stopped to think about it, I realized that as the person in charge of the brewery, there was no way Corinna would have shown a third party such confidential documents without consulting her lord first.

Now that I understood the Great Alchemist's blessings had been a product of her Sainthood, I wished I could just move on to the next step, but there was another problem: I still didn't know how to use the powers of the Saint.

The reason I read the diary nonstop for multiple days in a row was because I hoped something in it would let me at last figure it all out. I'd take anything, even the tiniest hint. However, I didn't make any progress. I didn't even find any particularly noteworthy description that gave me pause.

The moment I finished the diary, I stretched in my chair. The Great Alchemist had lovely, tidy handwriting, but reading her work for so long had made my eyes tired. I rubbed them with my hands and sighed.

Sunlight streamed through a window in the back of the room. Based on the length of the shadows, I guessed it was about three o'clock in the afternoon. I had a vague memory of hearing the bell chiming the time not too long ago.

I've just been reading, reading, reading since this morning. Maybe I ought to head outside for some fresh air? Well, no time like the present. I stood up from my chair.

"Oh? Heading out?" Corinna asked when I emerged from the back room.

"I was thinking I need a walk to clear my head."

"That might be a good idea." She smiled sympathetically.

I must have looked exhausted. She patted my back encouragingly as I left.

I headed for the area behind the castle, where I knew they kept a small field that the alchemists used to experiment with growing methods. It didn't smell as strongly of herbs as the brewery did, but being near it refreshed me for some reason, and in any case, it was a nice change of pace.

When I got to the field, I let out a sigh. I squatted down next to it and rested my chin in both hands as I gazed absentmindedly at the scenery. Since I was so low to the ground, the only thing I could see with any clarity were the herbs swaying in the breeze.

For a while, my head was empty and melancholy teased at my heart.

All in all, this investigation was a lot rougher going than I had imagined it would be. The Great Alchemist had written in great detail about her experiments, so I had hoped she would be similarly meticulous with her description of blessings and how they worked—but she wasn't. Not at all. Rather, the only things she wrote about in any like detail were the other necessary growing conditions and the lives of her people.

Hmm. Maybe there's something I'm overlooking, I thought as I gazed at the herbs while sifting through my memories of the diary.

She actually spent a lot of time writing about the people who lived in her father's domain, down to the minutia of their daily lives.

Now that I think about it, there were some people she wrote about especially frequently. That one guy in particular came up a whole bunch—it kind of sounded like he was her little brother?

She'd written about him rather extensively, actually. In fact, hadn't he kind of been the first person she had used the blessing for?

Specifically, she had originally focused on herb cultivation in order to combat a disease that was spreading in Klausner's Domain. The symptoms progressed slowly, but the afflicted person grew weaker and weaker until they finally passed. While the Great Alchemist strove to grow more and more potent herbs, her people continued to fall to the disease until it reached her brother, too. This had only inspired her to work harder.

As the herb she needed to save her people was difficult to obtain, she had thrown her resources into growing it instead of searching it out. Her gamble had paid off, and she was able to use the herbs she grew to make potions that rescued the life of her brother and the health of her people.

On the record of the day her brother's condition

began to improve, the ink of her words had been runny and blotched with signs of her relieved tears.

Yet nothing about this really stood out to me, at least not with regard to her powers. "Hmm, what a mystery."

Maybe the hint was in a part I'd accidentally skimmed? It wasn't like I could remember every single word in the diary, so it was possible. But would it be an event so trivial that I couldn't remember it?

No matter how I thought, I couldn't come up with an answer. Also, my legs were starting to feel numb, so I stood up. As I stretched my arms and my back, they made a popping sound. *Gosh*, I'd spent a lot of time reading that diary.

I wasn't sure I was feeling any more clearheaded, but I had been out for some time, so I felt compelled to head back.

I got up, and as I headed off, I heard some people talking loudly. I turned toward the noise and spotted the mercenary company coming toward the castle. There was something different about them today—something that troubled me. I strained to see what was going on, suddenly worried something serious had happened.

The second I spotted someone I knew in the crowd, I took it as an excuse to run over to them. As I got closer, I realized what was wrong. They were coming toward the castle from the direction of the forest, and most of them had some kind of injury. Some even had to lean on others to walk.

"Are you all right?!" I gasped as I approached Leonhardt—or Leo, as I'd started to call him even in my head.

His hard expression softened at the sight of me. "Oh? It's you, missy."

Most of the mercenaries blinked at me in confusion, unsure of who I was, but a couple smiled weakly when they recognized me—they were the ones who always came to pick up potions at the brewery. I heard one of the ones who recognized me explaining that to the others.

"Did you just come back from an expedition?" I asked.

"'Fraid so. We ran into some unusual beasties near the outer edge of the forest. Just finished killing the lot. We put up a good fight, but there were quite a few. Nearly did us in."

"Oh no! Are you guys going to be okay?"

"Yeah, yeah. We're in way better shape than we would be, thanks to your potions."

The other men chimed in with their agreement.

"So you're the one who made those potions?" asked one.

"You saved my life!" said another.

"Without that potion, I wouldn't be standing here right now."

"The effects of that potion I drank were amazing!"

Well at least that fifty-percent-bonus curse was good for *something*.

Once Leo outed me like that, I was surrounded by the mercenaries as they showered me with thanks. Although I was used to being around the Knights of the Third Order, being surrounded by these men—who were even more muscular and bulky—was a bit intimidating.

I worried my smile looked forced—I hoped they'd overlook it. Come on, they had to know how overwhelming they were!

"Please tell me you're off to get healed at the castle," I said to Leo.

"That we are. But I'm telling you, we got off easy with your help. Granted, some of us still need a little more treatment, but we'll be fine."

"Listen, come to the brewery, and I'll prepare a few more potions for you."

"Nah, we're not doing that badly. Slap on some bandages and we'll be good to go."

"Really? Some of you look kinda rough."

"Ah, I suppose there's no hiding it from you. Hmm, well, are you sure you don't think we can make do...?"

Leo rejected my idea out of hand, and I didn't get why at first—his people obviously needed the potions, even if he was being weirdly evasive about it. He scratched his head, a disconcerted expression on his face.

I frowned. He knew potions healed bodies faster than natural processes. He and his men were professionals.

Oh no—are they hesitating because of the herb shortage? Oh boy, I bet they give themselves a strict quota for how many potions they're allowed to use every day. I do make the same amount for them every time. Well...then why don't I heal them up using my magic instead?

Leo and his men were responsible for patrols that kept the whole domain safe, and that meant fighting monsters every day. It would be best for everyone if they could do their job in perfect health.

I had asked before if Klausner Castle had anyone who could use Healing Magic, but nope. I was surprised to hear this, considering this was the capital for a whole domain, but this dearth of skills seemed to be the norm everywhere in the countryside.

I supposed there were only a few people who could use magic in the first place, and even fewer of those who could use Healing Magic, and most of them went to the capital to join the Royal Magi Assembly. Also, I'd heard the members of the Royal Magi Assembly made way more money than those who worked in the countryside castle towns.

So, this was up to me.

"How about I heal all of you, then?" I asked.

"Hmm? Ah, Sei, I'm afraid your potions—"

"Um, no, I mean with magic."

"Huh?" Leo and the mercenaries all stared at me, flabbergasted. Well, I'd seen that coming. It had to be hard to imagine someone with Healing Magic was all the way out here.

Leo regained his composure and eyed me with suspicion. "I thought you were an alchemist."

"Uh..." How could I respond to that? It was true enough that I was a researcher at the Research Institute of Medicinal Flora, and I had skills in Pharmaceuticals. It would be okay to call myself an alchemist, right? "I am indeed an alchemist."

They continued to stare at me in silent disbelief. I tried to shrug it off. I had a feeling I'd lose if I engaged.

"Well, do you want me to heal you or not?" I asked.

Leo seemed to give up and just said, "Yes."

Once I got his permission, I started casting Heal on those nearby. Some mercenaries had pretty serious injuries, but nothing life-threatening, so I didn't need to give anyone priority.

Because Healing Magic was so rare, or perhaps I should say since there were so many who were having

Heal cast on them for the first time, they all watched the spell work its (literal) magic with sparkles in their eyes.

Considering the number of injured, my area-of-effect spell Area Heal would have been faster, but I opted for regular old Heal instead—it stood out less. Area-of-effect spells required a fairly high skill level. I had a feeling that if I used something that showy in a place where Healing Magic was already rare, it'd invite all sorts of headaches. Therefore, I tried to pull this off as subtly as possible.

However, all my smooth-operator confidence crumbled at a brief comment from Leo: "You're good at that."

"I am?"

"Yeah. I've seen a mage from the palace heal others before, but your spell looks more, I dunno, powerful."

"Th-thanks."

"If you can do this, I bet the knights will call on you later, too."

"Huh?"

"They had some injuries as well."

Oh no—was the Third Order okay?

"Yeah, we were traveling together on the way back," Leo went on. "They were in way worse shape than we were."

"They went far deeper in the forest than usual, so that's probably why," said one of the mercenaries.

"It's wild in there right now—way too many monsters. Gotta be fully prepared before you so much as set foot out in the field."

"Um, by knights, are you talking about the guys who came in from the capital?" I asked, shaking—it was a dumb question. I knew the answer. And yet I hoped...

"Of course. Who else?"

The mercenary's confirmation shot a chill down my spine.

And then, as always happened whenever I thought of the knights, I pictured Albert's smiling face.

And then I imagined a grim scene I had seen only once before.

"Area Heal!"

"Hey!" Leo cried out in surprise when I suddenly cast this spell, but his words didn't reach me.

My spell instantly healed all the mercenaries at once, but I didn't stay to see it. I didn't even turn back toward the voices that called to me as I dashed away, running as hard and as fast as I could toward the building where the knights were stationed.

When was the last time I ran with all my might? Am I faster than I used to be? I think so—I'm like Olympic-level fast, I thought deliriously as I kept moving my feet with all my strength.

I knew it wasn't really the time for such frivolous thoughts, but if I didn't think of *something*, I'd panic.

The mercenaries' words pounded in my head in time with my feet. The knights were hurt, even worse than the mercenaries had been. Just how bad was it?

I had seen them get injured before, obviously, back when I participated in that expedition near the capital. If they were only as wounded as they had been then, then I would make it in time. The abilities of the Royal Magi Assembly mages who had been with us had been sufficient to tend those hurts.

But if their condition was worse than those I'd just seen, which had been bad enough...! It was bad. It had to be.

Is he *all right?* I bit my lip at the sudden thought. *No. It doesn't matter what state he's in, so long as he's still alive. If he is, I'll heal him with everything I have.*

With renewed determination, I finally reached the quarters of the Knights of the Third Order. As it came into view, I also came across some of the knights, heading back toward their station in a wounded wave.

There were a staggering number of injuries. Nearly half of those I saw needed the support of their fellows.

I winced at the sight of it. The throng of injured filled the entry to the building.

One of the knights noticed me the second I arrived. "Sei!"

The other knights simultaneously looked up. Their haggard faces all turned to ones of relief.

"Are you all right?" I asked.

"Well as can be. As you can see, we didn't lose anyone."

I shivered with relief.

"They're working on treating the people inside and—"

"I'll go help!" I interrupted.

The knight thanked me with an apologetic look.

He didn't need to. Although I'd come to Klausner's Domain because I had an interest in the alchemist's holy land, I was also here to join the expeditions. It was only natural that I help treat everyone's wounds.

I responded with a brief smile and went on my way.

The entrance hall was crowded, but the men who noticed me passing made way for me. The inside of the main hall was just as crowded. The handful of mages from the Royal Magi Assembly who had come with us were sitting on chairs with lines of injured people waiting to see them. They were caring for those who could stand on their own.

Spread out behind them, sitting or lying down along the walls, were those who were worst off. Other mages walked among them, using Healing Magic one at a time.

But where's Albert? I should check in with him and see where he thinks I'll be of most use. I frantically surveyed the hall, but I didn't spot his familiar blond hair, not anywhere. *Is he not back yet? Or...*

A sinking feeling spread through my chest.

But wait, no, that knight just told me there weren't any deaths. I shook my head back and forth to dispel the evil thought.

As I resumed searching for Albert, I happened to make eye contact with a knight who beckoned me over. He was part of a cluster of people. *Is that where Albert is?*

I rushed over and found Albert sitting on a chair in the middle of the group.

Is something wrong with him?

He had a somewhat dazed, languid look. I couldn't see his expression clearly, though, since his face was turned down.

"Lord Hawke!" I called out his name and froze.

A servant was patting Albert's head with a white cloth. A small stain, dark and red, spread over it.

A head injury? Oh no! The blood drained from my face. *That's not good. That's not good at all. I have to heal him!*

The moment that thought slashed through my mind, a familiar sensation seeped out from my heart. "What the?!"

"Sei!"

Huh?! Why?! I panicked—I had no idea what was going on, but I couldn't stop the magic overflowing from within me.

White and gold magic poured out of me and into the air, gradually filling the entire hall. The knights cried out in surprise at the sight of it.

O-oh dear. What do I do? You know what, fine. I suppose for now... My confused train of thought came to a stop as I remembered what I needed to do—what I wanted to do. *That's right. I'm here to heal everyone. I have to heal* him.

Right as I thought that, the magic activated, and it was like all the light, my magic, reacted at once. A powerful radiance filled every inch of the hall. My vision went completely white. Once the light receded, everyone had been healed, just like I had wished for.

When everyone could see again, cheers of joy cascaded through the hall.

"Sei?" came a soft voice from just in front of me.

"Oh... Lord Hawke. Are you all right?" I was at a loss, as my sudden show of magic had disoriented me, but his voice snapped me back to reality.

Thankfully, his injury was healed now, too.

"Yes..." He frowned. "Though I don't believe I was injured all that badly."

"Y-you weren't? I thought you hurt your head."

"I'm fine, I promise. It looked worse than it was because of the bleeding."

The servant removed their hand from Albert's head to show me that the bleeding had stopped. Although I knew I'd healed everyone, I was relieved to see it.

"By the way, did you just...?" Albert trailed off.

I nodded before he finished his sentence. "Yes."

Everyone knew what he wanted to ask, and why he couldn't quite say it out loud—he wanted to ask if I had used the power of the Saint.

But what in the world had caused me to use it *now* of all times? It wasn't like I had intentionally triggered the power—it wasn't anything like when I used Healing Magic.

Nevertheless, something had summoned it forth.

As I thought it over, I suddenly remembered a passage in the Great Alchemist's diary. She had first used her powers when she was in a panic over her brother's worsening condition.

Was it panic? Was that the answer? Or was it more about the context? I had been incredibly upset when I saw Albert injured. I'd felt the same way about a similar thing happening back in the western forest as well.

But what about when I had first used it back at the institute? At that moment, I had been frustrated by my inability to find a way to make stronger potions. However, if frustration was all it took, I should have been able to use the power at the Royal Magi Assembly practice grounds as well. Yuri's insistence on standing beside me while I practiced had certainly put that kind of pressure on me. I had been plenty frustrated then, even panicked at times. And yet, I hadn't used the magic.

If it wasn't panic, and it wasn't frustration, then what in the world caused the power to activate?

"—Sei?" A voice called my name over and over and snapped me out of my reverie.

Albert was looking up at me with worry, seeing as I hadn't responded to him despite him saying my name, er, multiple times.

"Ah, I'm sorry. I got lost in thought."

"About the Saint's power?"

"Yeah... I still don't know how it works, even now, seconds after I did it."

"Hmm." Albert put a hand to his chin and sank into thought.

The nearby knights also started thinking it over.

And you know what? I was grateful, intensely so, that so many people were trying to help me solve this mystery—especially because sometimes you figure something out when someone just happens to ask you the right idle question. The way they all started throwing out ideas made me feel like I belonged.

Belonged... Belonging. When I thought about it, that time when I first used the power back at the institute, I had also been thinking about everyone in the institute and in the Third Order. *Could it be that thinking about the people in my in-groups—that sense of belonging and caring—is the trigger? Hmm. That doesn't seem like quite enough, though.*

However, I had a gut feeling that I was on the right track.

If I remember correctly, back at the institute, I was... As I thought back as best as I could to the very first time I had used the golden magic, I felt a change within me. It was strangely...like an ache. It left me momentarily surprised. When I stopped thinking so hard, the feeling subsided. I frowned.

And then I realized. My face went crimson.

"What's wrong?" Albert asked.

"O-oh, it's nothing."

I couldn't find it in me to tell him the truth.

Nooooo. There's no way I can tell you, even if you do keep looking at me like that! Because... Because... How am I supposed to explain that thinking about you *was what made me use the power?! It's way too embarrassing! There's no way! Absolutely no way I can tell you!*

Behind the Scenes III

CLOUDS GATHERED in the sky over Klausner's Domain, letting just a trace of light enter Lord Daniel Klausner's office, which was quite dark, even though sunset was yet hours away. In this gloom, there was only the sound of the lord's pen scratching across paper until it was interrupted by a knock on the door.

The servant on duty went to the door as Daniel continued to work. He heard Corinna announce herself and nodded at the servant to let her in.

"Pardon me for the intrusion," Corinna said as she entered the room and bowed.

Daniel prompted her to take a seat on one of the sofas in front of his desk. He had just reached a good stopping point, so he set down his pen and moved to the sofa opposite Corinna.

Here, they sat together in silence.

A few moments later, the servant brought some tea. After placing a cup in front of each of them, Daniel ordered the servant to leave. The servant said nothing as he left the room; this sort of order was not uncommon during Corinna's visits. The other servants and officials cleared the room as well.

Once Daniel and Corinna were alone, Corinna spoke. "Today, I gave the Saint the Great Alchemist's diary."

"I see. And did anything come of it?"

"Not yet. It seemed to remind her of something, though she wouldn't tell me what."

Daniel put a hand to his chin as he pondered this.

Corinna knew that look. Daniel wasn't wasting time fantasizing about what he hoped might happen; he was contemplating what their next move would be. She quietly waited for him to speak again.

The diary Corinna had shown Sei held the greatest secret of Klausner's Domain. It revealed that the Saint's abilities extended far beyond the slaying of monsters.

A king of many generations past had ordered all records of the Saint's special abilities disposed of in order to protect her. However, the Great Alchemist had lived in the days before that decree.

By all rights, that diary should have been destroyed.

However, the lord of Klausner's Domain of that era had hidden it instead. He had allowed many other records of her achievements to be burned, but as medicinal herb cultivation was his people's foremost industry, this document was precious, even vital, and the lord opted to preserve it, even if it meant defying the king's order.

While the most damning part of the text described the blessings required to cultivate specific rare herbs, the diary also went in-depth into the various techniques the Great Alchemist had developed to establish the local industry. It was an invaluable resource when it came to determining how best to cultivate new products. In other words, the Lord Klausner of that time had saved the diary for the sake of future generations.

Furthermore, as the diary never described the Saint's powers in detail—especially not compared to other contemporary documents—the Lord Klausner felt more justified in his decision. Nevertheless, he had known better than to publicly disobey the king, hence the secrecy with which the diary was kept. To this day, only the lords of Klausner and the head alchemists in the castle's brewery were ever told of the diary's existence.

This is all to say that Daniel had chosen to show this precious, dangerous document to Sei with an ulterior motive—a critically important one.

"You say it reminded her of something. Do you mean you think she can once more bless the fields?"

"I apologize, my lord. She has thus far said nothing specific."

"Then we may not be able to revive the fields, after all." Daniel crossed his arms, and the crease in his brow deepened.

There were, in truth, two reasons for the current herb shortage in Klausner's Domain.

First, due to the increase in monsters, the people had become unable to gather medicinal herbs growing in the forest, and neither were they able to properly harvest the fields close to it.

Second, the number of herbs they could grow in the once-blessed fields had significantly decreased.

The herbs grown in the blessed fields could be divided into two types: herbs that simply grew more easily in blessed soil and herbs that *required* the blessing.

Among this former group were staple ingredients in mid-grade HP potions and the like. They had grown well before, but a few years ago, the harvest had begun to gradually decrease. Now, the people of the domain could reliably expect to harvest about sixty percent of what they had in their heyday.

As for the herbs that required blessings, the domain had long since been unable to grow these at all, and they had come to rely on gathering these herbs in the forest to meet demand.

The blessing in these fields had lasted since the days of the Great Alchemist's original casting. They had never been blessed by any other Saint since, even though that original blessing had happened so many generations in the past, and even though the threat of the miasma had continued to grow.

However, it was evident to Daniel and Corinna that the effects of her blessing had weakened.

When the decline first began, Corinna and her alchemists had conducted all manner of surveys to see if they could discern the cause. Their results were clear: nothing in the world had changed dramatically enough to reflect the problems they were seeing.

As they continued their investigations, the miasma in Salutania grew denser and denser, and all during that time, the kingdom couldn't find the Saint, the only one who could purify the miasma. Just when the kingdom was deciding to perform the Saint Summoning Ritual, Daniel and Corinna concluded the effects of the Great Alchemist's blessing on Klausner's Domain might have finally run out.

At this conclusion, Daniel was at his wit's end. Who but the Great Alchemist could bless fields? There had never been any mention of anyone with similar gifts. Specifically, the diary mentioned the blessing magic was golden in color, and Daniel had never seen nor heard of such power before.

Unable to find a solution to the real problem, he had made ample use of his mercenaries and focused on gathering as many herbs as possible from the forest to offset the deficit in the fields. But this could only ever be a stopgap, and they could not simply pray that an alternative industry would spring up overnight.

Just as Daniel was about to lose hope in the future of his land, he heard a rumor from the capital: the Saint had participated in an expedition into Ghoshe Forest, and there she had let loose a purifying wave of golden magic.

When Daniel heard this, he realized there might still be hope for his people.

You might imagine he should have thought of this sooner, but the fact was that although some people remembered a Saint had once been born in Klausner's Domain, as you know, much of the information on her life had been destroyed. Furthermore, few could connect her to the tales of the Great Alchemist. Even Daniel frequently forgot the two were connected, as he and his people remembered this remarkable woman more for her agricultural brilliance than for her Sainthood.

Then was this golden magic a power that belonged to the Saint? Daniel wondered. After consulting with Corinna, he decided to request the Saint visit his lands. Officially, he would call on her to slay monsters, but his true goal would be to beseech her to bless the fields again. He still didn't know for certain if she could do such a thing, but this was his last hope.

Though he had his people attempt to gather intel on the current Saint, he learned very little about her as a person, though his people reported that she had been working at the Research Institute of Medicinal Flora at the palace due to personal interest. Her work there gave him hope she would take further interest in Klausner's Domain, which might pave the way to asking her to bless the fields.

Daniel's heart had lightened at the thought.

When Daniel wrote the letter requesting the knightly Orders be dispatched to his domain, he was still unsure whether to specifically request the Saint as well. He ultimately neglected to do so, as he feared any specific questions might lead to the revelation that he and his people held illicit knowledge of the Saint's abilities. Therefore, he rolled the dice and prayed she would be sent to them regardless.

A short time after sending the letter, the response arrived. Daniel's gamble had paid off: the palace wrote that the Saint would be dispatched as well. Now all Daniel had to do was to, somehow, convince the Saint to bless the fields—something she had no idea he hoped she would do.

First, Corinna tried to indirectly determine the nature of the Saint's powers, but the Saint mentioned no abilities other than purifying miasma. Daniel didn't lose hope. He understood the palace might have told the Saint to withhold the true extent of her power, and that she might not even know the true breadth of her abilities. However, judging from her lack of caution when making her unusually potent potions, Daniel guessed it was more likely the latter.

After much consideration, he decided to show the Saint the Great Alchemist's diary. He left the timing of this to Corinna, telling her only to report to him after she did.

Corinna was now in his office to follow through on that order.

"She seemed to recognize the part about the golden magic," Corinna said.

"Really?!" Daniel's expression brightened.

"I heard the magic she used in the western forest was golden as well."

"As did I. You know, the color of magic is typically an indication of elemental affinity. That must mean this gold color indicates the powers of the Saint, just as we predicted."

"I do believe so. I've seen many elemental effects in my time, but never a golden hue."

Since the Saint's arrival in Klausner's Domain, Daniel had heard rumors from the people of the castle, especially from the alchemists who worked in the brewery, that the Saint was every bit as obsessed with medicinal herbs as the Great Alchemist had been. Even if she didn't know anything about blessings, there was reason to hope she would become interested in them after reading the Great Alchemist's diary.

We might just be able to achieve our original objective after all, Daniel thought.

"Well. I believe we can dare to hope," Daniel said.

"Hmph. She will need to bless the fields in order to cultivate that herb she's been searching for. I am confident she will soon attempt to perform blessings all on her own."

"That would be most welcome."

Daniel smiled, and that lingering sense of anguish within him began to lessen. But what Daniel didn't know was that the Saint couldn't yet use her powers of her own volition. Both Daniel and Corinna assumed that Sei was in full command of her abilities, especially after what they'd heard of her journey to the western forest.

Only a few people knew the truth. Naturally, they hid it, hoping to save the people of Salutania from unnecessary fear.

However, the star of fortune shone down on Daniel, for a few days after this conversation, Sei managed to call on her Saintly powers again. You might say it was profound luck—or you might say it had something to do with the Great Alchemist's blessing upon Klausner's Domain and a final flare of that fading strength.

ACT
6
Discovery

I FLOPPED MY UPPER HALF over the writing desk in my quarters and sighed exaggeratedly. I had been holed up in my room all morning doing experiments, but the results were just as I expected. And by that, I meant my expectations had been super dang low. To tell you the truth, I wished I hadn't been right.

The day before, I had used my Saintly powers at the Order's quarters. I had been absolutely shocked, as it had just happened all of a sudden, but at least I'd managed to heal everybody, so I couldn't say boo to that. I was also happily, finally cognizant of what I needed in order to trigger my powers.

This was a relief in a lot of ways. For one, now I could make a certain grand magus lay off with all the pressure he'd been putting on me. That was cause for celebration indeed.

There was just one teeny little problem—i.e., the thing I needed to do in order to make my power work. Argh! Why did it have to be linked to Knight Commander Albert?!

I had been experimenting like crazy all morning. I was totally justified in this, too! I mean, Albert wasn't the *only* person I'd thought about when I summoned magic those other times. Like the first time, I'd also been thinking about Jude, and Johan, and the other researchers, and the knights, and—well, suffice to say, thinking about them did jack squat this time around.

I dreaded doing it, but I finally forced myself to focus on Albert, and...the moment I pushed through my embarrassment and clearly pictured him, the Saint's power surged up inside me. Easy as pie. Even more damningly, the second I wished for the churning within me to stop, it stopped. Great! Now I was getting used to it.

To tell the truth, if I had been the only one in my quarters, I would have started wailing and pounding my fists on the desk. I mean, this meant that every time I wanted to use my Saintly powers, I had to think about gorgeous, thoughtful, sweet, warm, wonderful Albert. What kind of absolutely unholy, unjust, and totally uncalled for torture was this?!

However, Mary and several other maids were with me. I couldn't just roll around the floor with both hands covering my steaming red face, no matter how much I wanted to. The best I could do was let out that tremendous sigh.

"Lady Sei, perhaps you should consider taking a break?" Mary's anxious voice came from behind my face-planted head.

"Thank you. I think I will." I lifted my head from the desk and glanced back to find her smiling at me. She had already placed a perfectly prepared cup of tea on the table by the sofas.

Well, how can I say no to that? She'd also prepared some sweets that went well with the local herbal tea, and there were some sandwiches and fruits as well. In fact, I had seen this spread before—it was just like what I usually made back at the institute.

I glanced again at Mary, who smiled and said, "Please have a bite to eat as well."

My stomach growled. It occurred to me then that I had started experimenting as soon as I got dressed, and I hadn't actually eaten anything at all since then. When I thought about it a little more, I realized I hadn't eaten anything for dinner the night before, either—on account of how the second I'd returned from the Order's quarters, I had sequestered myself in my bedroom.

Normally, I ate three meals a day. But here I was, having ignored my dinner and left myself grimacing at my desk since the crack of dawn. I must have worried Mary. At least, that was the feeling I got when I saw all that food on the table. She probably thought that if I saw this familiar spread, I might finally work up an appetite.

I felt bad as I picked up one of the sandwiches, but as I did, I suddenly felt the incredible pangs of hunger. The sandwich was gone in the blink of an eye.

As I reached for one of the pastries next, I noticed the maids were sagging with relief. I hadn't just worried Mary. *Sorry, everyone...*

After I finished devouring pretty much everything and was washing it all down with some tea, Mary told me some people had come calling while I was holing myself up. There was a whole list of visitors I'd turned away, and the longer it got, the more ashamed I became—I had freaked them out, hadn't I?

Since I'd never returned to the brewery, even Corinna had stopped by to check in on me. Albert—considerate Albert—had come as well.

However, Mary had tactfully received them all in my stead, having determined from my behavior that I wasn't ready to see anybody at all. I was eternally grateful to her, especially as Corinna and Albert were the last people I would have wanted to see me in that state.

After using my powers, I had pretty much fled the Order's quarters. I had heard Albert calling out to me as I did, but I had ignored him.

Knowing him, he probably would've been downright anxious about me. But I...I just didn't know how to face him.

The first time we met, I'd instantly recognized that he was my type, looks-wise. And ugh, I know that's kind of shallow! The real problem was that every time we'd met after that, he had been unfailingly gentle and terribly kind. But whatever I was feeling right now was new—I'd never felt this overwhelmed before.

Would I still be able to act like a normal human being around him the next time we met? I didn't like my odds. But it wasn't like I could keep avoiding him. We had a job to do, and we had to do it together, or the monsters in Klausner's Domain wouldn't be going anywhere.

That's right. Yeah. A job. I can't just neglect it. I'm just going to keep it professional, and then maybe I won't feel so devastatingly awkward when I have to think about him when I use the Saint's magic. Yeah! Maybe I'm not a hundred percent positive I can do this, but I'll just have to give it a shot.

"Thanks for the food," I said, standing and nodding to the maids.

"Do you have any plans for the rest of the day?" asked Mary.

"I think I'm going to go to the brewery."

"Very well."

Corinna had come to check on me the day before as well, so I felt compelled to let her know I was okay.

Plus, there was still the matter of the blessings to discuss. I wasn't entirely clear on what they were, but I could now wield my powers at will. I could commence with the experiments, and I had all sorts in mind. If they went well, I'd at last be able to acquire the special herb I was looking for. I was getting excited just thinking about it.

First, I need to figure out just what a blessing looks like... and then I need to get Corinna's permission to experiment on some fields.

"Are you feeling better now?" Corinna asked me when I arrived at the brewery.

"Yes. I'm so sorry to have worried you." I bowed.

"Well. I'm just glad you're all right."

Pleasantries and apologies done with, I dove into the important stuff. We headed into the back room to keep it discreet, and she seemed to catch my drift right away, perhaps because I spoke in a hushed tone. I assumed this was all rather confidential information, and we therefore wanted to avoid hashing it out in a room packed with other people.

"You want to run experiments, you say?"

"Yeah. Although first I'd like to review the Great Alchemist's notes again."

"What's your first step after that?"

"I'm thinking I'll pick a specific kind of herb to experiment with. If you can part with them, I'd like to borrow some flowerpots or something similar."

"Why flowerpots?"

"Well, it'd be pretty bad if I messed up, right? I don't want to risk hurting a whole field."

"Ah, right you are. Very well, I'll get some for you."

"Thank you, Corinna."

Given that I'd once enchanted—blessed—er, done something to a whole garden of herbs back at the Research Institute of Medicinal Flora, I was feeling pretty optimistic, but better safe than sorry, right?

Corinna told me she'd have everything ready for me in a few hours, so until then, I settled back in with the Great Alchemist's records.

Sure enough, in a matter of hours, Corinna had everything ready for my experiments. We headed to the location she had set up for me, which was near the herb fields behind the castle that they used for experimenting.

Corinna had set up a multitiered rack of wood. Five unglazed clay pots sat on it, already full of soil, but there were more pots that nearby gardeners were filling as well.

As Corinna and I approached, the eldest of the gardeners turned to us. "This is pretty much everything we've got right now. Will you be needing any more?"

"No, I'm sure these will be more than enough," said Corinna. "If it goes wrong, we might ask you to change out the soil or some such."

"Righty-o. Let us know if you need anything else."

"Thanks."

Corinna and the gardeners were on pretty casual terms with one another, seeing as they helped her out a lot with cultivation of the fields, especially the trickier specimens.

The gardener got back to work, and soon all of the pots had been filled. They left us with cheerful nods and smiles and went on to their other responsibilities.

Corinna confirmed they had all left before saying, "Time to get started, then."

"Yeah." I headed over to the rack, pausing when something occurred to me. "What about the seeds?"

"Here." Corinna pulled out a small bag filled with seeds

from her skirt pocket. "This species grows the quickest of all those we have in stock."

And did this kind require blessings in order to grow in the local climate? I double-checked with Corinna in a low voice, as the gardeners were still in hearing distance. She nodded in confirmation.

She was thinking about this as carefully as I was. Thank goodness.

As Corinna passed me the seeds, she quietly described the herb they would grow into. Running over the necessary conditions for growing this herb in my mind, I set about planting it. The gardeners had provided everything I needed except for the blessing—fertilizer and the like—so all I had to do was properly place the seed in the damp earth.

Once I did, I placed my hands on the pot and thought for a moment. Now I just needed to use my powers. But how? There was a difference between summoning the power and actually wielding it.

When I had done this back at the research institute, I had prayed for the herbs already growing to become more potent. This situation was a bit different, as these herbs wouldn't grow on their own without my help. So should I pray for their growth? Their healthy growth? *I guess I'll give that a try first.*

I took a deep breath and summoned my power—then froze. I'd just remembered how much thinking-about-Albert this operation required. I started blushing, and furiously at that.

"Something the matter?" Corinna asked, eyeing me dubiously.

"N-no, I'm all right," I answered hastily. There was absolutely, positively no way I could tell her the truth.

I zeroed in on the pot again. *Ugh. C'mon. Time to focus on the work. Focus, focus. Be a professional, Sei!*

I pulled myself together and forced myself to think of Albert, just like I had all morning. Magic power roared through my chest, and this time, I didn't tell it to stop. I let it overflow.

As I wanted the magic to feed into the pot in my hands, I tried focusing on the flow of my magic just like I did when I channeled my power to cast Healing Magic. How lucky that the grand magus had spent all that time tutoring me on exactly this.

As I anticipated, a white mist shot through with golden sparkles spread across the soil in the pot.

"Oh, my," Corinna said with admiration as she watched.

Would this be enough? I hoped so. I *prayed* so. I prayed for the plant to grow, and the magic flickering over the soil reacted. It glowed, becoming more luminous before it burst in a brilliant little flash. Golden sparkles flowed out over the rim of the pot.

"Did it work?" Corinna asked.

"I...I'm not sure. *Something* happened."

"I suppose we'll find out in a bit, depending on whether or not the seed sprouts. Let's check back on it later."

"Yeah...that sounds about right."

"This one's next."

"Huh?"

She handed me another small bag.

Ohhh. Welp. From the number of pots, I had assumed I would be doing different kinds of prayers on the same type of seeds, but instead, Corinna wanted me to try using my power on different types. I did stop her to explain my original notion, and she agreed that this was a more solidly methodical way to do it, so we combined our methods. In the end, I tried different prayers in sequence on a whole batch of different types.

I'll have you know that it was transcendentally mortifying to have to think of Albert every time I used the magic, though.

"Good job." Corinna patted me on the shoulder when I reached the end of the pots.

"Thank you." I smiled.

"The fastest-growing of these seeds should sprout in about two to three days."

"I'll stop by to check on them tomorrow, just in case."

"Good idea. Well, let's head back in for now."

We turned to make our way to the brewery together. We had only just reached the castle when I spotted Leo headed in our direction. He noticed us, grinned, and broke into a run to reach us faster.

I looked at Corinna in confusion. From her puzzled expression, she didn't know what had prompted this reaction of his, either.

I assumed he had some business with Corinna, but it turned out that wasn't the case. As soon as Leo reached us, he seized me by both shoulders. "Join my mercenary company!"

"Wh-what?" I was stunned by the sudden invitation. Had he really just asked me what I thought he had? What in the world? "Uh, what makes you say that?"

"Because I want you to be part of my company!"

"Oh... Uh, I really have no idea where this is coming from. What made you want to invite me?"

Leo was incredibly animated as he explained himself: it all came down to how I had healed his men the day before.

As I noted previously, very few people could use magic, and even fewer possessed Healing Magic, especially in the countryside. And here I had appeared before Leo and his company with a full display of my power. Having someone who could use Healing Magic in his company would improve the survival rate of his men by a heretofore unimaginable degree.

Also, there was the little fact that I'd panicked and used the Area Heal spell, which required a rather high level in Holy Magic. Therefore, Leo had deduced I was exceptionally skilled. He assured me that being an alchemist was, simply put, a waste of my talents.

Leo's words made Corinna's gaze go chilly, and she said in a cool tone, "Hold on a minute. What do you mean being an alchemist would be a waste of her talents?"

A drop of sweat ran down Leo's temple, but despite Corinna's menacing look, he stood his ground. "Oh, uh, I wasn't trying to diminish the work you alchemists do. It's just that her talent's exceptional. Know what I mean?"

"I'm aware of a mage's worth," Corinna sniffed. "Listen, I understand your interest, but you're going to have to give up on recruiting Sei."

"Eh? Why?!"

Corinna and Leo talked at each other as if I weren't even there. But, well, Corinna was right, I had no intention of joining Leo's company. So, I just continued to quietly watch their exchange. I had come from the capital, after all. I wasn't going to stay in Klausner's Domain forever.

Plus...if I left...

Just then, the temperature of the air around us dropped several degrees, as if a cold wind had sliced by and decided to stick around.

"What do you think you're doing?" Everyone turned to look past Leo at the person who had spoken.

Corinna's chilly gaze didn't even hold a candle to the frigid glare this man was giving Leo. I was suddenly sure the temperature drop hadn't been my imagination.

Um...I think you need to get a hold of your magic, buddy. Maybe do some drills? Ha ha...ha... This thought danced around in my head, desperately trying to help me escape the reality of my situation.

Albert was standing behind Leo, glaring at him with blue eyes like icicles.

On seeing Albert, Leo's own aura instantly sharpened as well. "Apologies, milord. We were merely having a pleasant conversation."

"Is that so? Then how long do you plan to keep hold of her shoulders?"

Huh? You know, I think that's the first time I've ever heard Leo be so stiff and formal. He sounds a bit weird! Oh, wait. I-I guess it must be because Albert's a noble and

all, I thought, my mind racing as Albert walked over to us. He very deliberately peeled Leo's hands from my shoulders.

As he did, Leo's aura grew all the more threatening.

"And just what were you talking about?" Albert demanded.

"Nothing of importance, milord."

"Are you kidding? You were just asking Sei to join your mercenary company," Corinna snapped.

"Granny!" Leo grimaced at Corinna.

Corinna sniffed, totally nonchalant.

However, despite Leo's panic, Albert's mood seemed to soften upon hearing this. Maybe he'd been afraid Leo had other intentions?

"Sei will not be joining your company," Albert said.

"And why're you the one who gets to decide that?" said Leo, breaking with his earlier stiffness. "I don't see how what Sei does is any of your business."

"It is, in fact, entirely my business. She came with us from the capital, after all."

"Eh? Wait, you mean she's one of the palace's mages? Then what's she doing making potions in the brewery all day?"

Uh, well, it's a hobby—or, actually, it's my job! And I'm not one of the mages, Leo, come on! I thought.

As I frowned up at him, some thought seemed to occur to Leo. His eyes widened, and his mouth fell open just a tad. "Hold up. Are *you* the Saint?"

"Watch your tone," Corinna snapped.

Leo stared at me, utterly dazed, and I tilted my head, a bit perplexed...until I realized that it was me. I was the problem.

Oops. Did I forget to tell him?

All right, all right. Perhaps I'd neglected to share that little detail. Call it force of habit!

The Saint's
Magic Power is
Omnipotent

Short Story

A FEW DAYS BEFORE Sei and the Knights of the Third Order departed for Klausner's Domain, Albert visited the Valdec family villa in the capital.

As he passed through the gates and neared the front door, a butler came out to receive him with an elegant bow. Albert dismounted from his horse and another servant came out as per usual to take it.

"Welcome. Thank you for coming," the butler greeted him.

"Sorry for all the trouble each time."

"Please, don't mention it."

The butler took Albert straight to the room Johan was waiting in.

"You're here sooner than I thought." Johan stood up to receive Albert as soon as the man stepped into the room.

"Well, we have everything pretty much prepared already."

They sat on the sofas facing each other, and a maid set out a light meal along with some cutlery on the table between them.

"Do you have enough potions? If you're not sure, we could always make more."

"We're all right. We've got more than enough, including an allotment for what we'll use along the way."

"If you say so."

"And if we run low, we'll just get more at our destination."

The butler poured wine into their glasses, then Johan waved a hand to dismiss him. Once the staff left, the two men raised their glasses in a toast. Now that they were alone, they could talk without fear of prying eyes and ears.

Johan took a sip of his wine and said, "That you can. If you can acquire the ingredients, you should ask Sei to make them. I'm sure she'd happily do so for you."

"Oh, I'd rather not bother her with anything like that..."

"I know." Johan grinned at Albert's flustered expression.

Albert had, in fact, been planning on purchasing more potions so long as they were available. He wanted to avoid asking Sei to do any extra work. And of course, Johan knew that.

Nevertheless, Johan happily implied Albert ought to use Sei for all she was worth, because he wanted to tease his friend. Albert picked up on this and made a face. "Please, don't mock me about this."

"Sorry, sorry."

Albert glared at Johan, who was stifling a laugh, before draining his own glass.

A few moments later, Johan managed to regain his composure and finished his glass as well. He then refilled both of their cups. "Well, if it does ever look like you're going to run out, I'm sure Sei will just make more for you even if you don't ask. You know how she is."

"She works too hard."

"I think so, too, you know. I tell her to take days off, but I think working is her idea of taking a break."

"I suppose she did say she doesn't work nearly as much in this world as she did in the one she came from..."

It had been approximately a year since Sei's summoning. Albert and Johan were always telling her to stop working so hard, but she denied that she was every single time they brought it up.

They sighed simultaneously, likely thinking the same thing.

Perhaps the problem was that she lived where she worked. Or maybe it was that the research institute's employees largely thought of research as their hobby, and Sei wasn't the only one who spent her off days pursuing more research projects. Being surrounded by such people meant Sei could brush off Johan and Albert's warnings and keep pushing herself whenever the impulse took her.

"Even when she does leave the institute, she always winds up making something new," Albert murmured.

"I keep catching her in the kitchen," said Johan.

"I suppose cooking might seem like a nice change of pace from her regular work."

Sei did occasionally spend her off days on formulating her personal cosmetics as well. Also, both the researchers *and* the chefs looked forward to Sei's kitchen concoctions, so Johan couldn't exactly ban her from the dining hall.

Not to mention, Sei always cooked new recipes on her days off, often because she was teaching the chefs how to make them. Every time she did this, she would write the recipe—ingredients and all—and reference that memo while instructing the chefs as they worked. At times, she paused in the middle of her work to warn the chefs about tricky steps and so forth. Therefore, the teaching made the cooking process take longer than if Sei were to just make it for herself.

Notably, because Sei didn't see cooking as work, she was a little resistant to letting it eat into her research time. Therefore, she really only brought these new recipes into the kitchen on her...days...off...

"Oh no!" Johan suddenly let out a moan, head hanging.

"What's wrong?" Albert asked in alarm.

"It's just...it just occurred to me. She'll be with you for the time being."

"What about it?"

"Her cooking. Her cooking!" Johan cradled his head in his hands.

If Sei was leaving the capital, she was taking all those recipes in her head with her. Johan had never been that particular about food before, but he adored trying every unfamiliar dish Sei threw together.

Part of it was that everything Sei made was utterly delicious, but the other part was that Johan was, at heart, a researcher, and he simply loved getting to experience unusual things.

While the chefs could make every recipe Sei had thus far shared with them, and they regularly offered her recipes on the dining hall menu, Sei's absence would mean a temporary moratorium on new additions to that menu.

The past year had seen Johan grow accustomed to Sei's steady introduction of fascinating new dishes, so the realization that he wouldn't be able to indulge in her repertoire for a while was a painful one, to say the least.

"You'll still get her recipes at the dining hall, won't you? What are you so depressed about?"

"But what about the ones she hasn't yet taught the chefs? I want to try every dish she knows!"

"Well, not much you can do about that."

"You're only so nonchalant because you're not going to be deprived."

"She's not coming along to cook for us, you realize."

"You never know."

"Do you think there will just happen to be a kitchen Sei can use whenever she wants? She's going as the *Saint*. They're not going to let her esteemed personage anywhere near the castle kitchens."

Very few people of high social status could cook in the Kingdom of Salutania. The higher their status, the less likely they were to know how—and all for the sake of keeping up their noble appearance.

Sei wasn't that type of stickler, but as the Saint, her social status was equal to the king's, perhaps even higher. Albert had a feeling that if Sei said she wanted to cook while they were in Klausner's Domain, the people of the castle, who didn't know her eccentricities, would do their damnedest to stop her. And he couldn't imagine Sei putting her foot down about it in that situation.

"You'll be on the road as well," Johan noted. "I heard how she cooked for everyone in the western forest."

"True, but there are only so many things you can do outside of a kitchen. I doubt we'll get to enjoy something like you'd be hoping for."

Albert shot Johan an exasperated look as his friend continued to hang his head. He couldn't deny that there was a good chance that Sei would cook for them during an expedition if given the chance.

However, the options on the road were indeed pretty limited. Sei could put together a soup or roast meat—which was exactly what she had done on prior expeditions—but that was the extent. There were only so many kinds of ingredients they could bring, too, so Albert doubted there was any way Sei would actually make something like Johan was pining for.

However, at the time, Albert hadn't really internalized what it meant to be going to the alchemist's holy land. Klausner's Domain was known for its vast fields of herbs, including those that couldn't be found in the capital. There was no guarantee Sei wouldn't make something new with those unique flora.

Albert only really figured this out after the fact, too—i.e., when they got back to the capital and Johan complained at length upon hearing that Sei had indeed devised a new recipe in Klausner's Domain.

Afterword

HELLO, THIS IS Yuka Tachibana. It's been a while. Thank you so much for buying *The Saint's Magic Power is Omnipotent,* Volume Three.

They say that time flies like an arrow, but it's actually been a whole year since Volume Two came out. I apologize for the long wait. It really felt like the whole year flew by in a flash.

I would like to thank my editor, W, at Kadokawa Books for adjusting the schedule as needed when things were so busy. Editor W and so many others have helped me so much ever since we first negotiated the publication of this series. I really owe a lot to the editing department. Thank you so much.

During this past year, *The Saint's Magic Power is Omnipotent* was turned into a manga series as well. The artist is Azuki Fuji-sensei. Thank you to everyone working on the manga side, too!

On top of drawing beautiful art, Fuji-sensei pulled the original story together in a tremendously satisfying way. When I first saw the completed manuscript, I was utterly absorbed in reading it. I only remembered at the end that I was supposed to be checking over the contents! Sei is adorable, and of course Albert and the rest of the men are wonderfully handsome as well. I'm in agony every time I read these manuscripts. Sei is just too cute for words.

Sorry, I just get way too fired up when I remember Sei during my favorite scenes!

You can find this wonderful version of the story on sites that host manga such as ComicWalker, pixiv Comic, and Nico Nico Seiga. You can read some of the chapters for free on these sites, so please take a look if you're interested. By the way, I especially adore Sei in Chapter 2, Part 2. It was so cute how Sei pretended not to hear Jude's voice. (I can't believe I'm saying that again!)

This makes my fourth afterword, if you include the one I wrote for the manga, so I'm not sure what to write here. How about I talk a bit about what happened in this volume as well as what's to come? There will be some spoilers, like there were in Volume Two's afterword, so please be sure to finish the whole book before continuing.

Now that we've gotten deeper into the story, the time has come for Sei to head out to the countryside. The Saint was originally summoned in order to cleanse the miasma that had spread across the kingdom, so you could say that her principal occupation is traveling across the land in order to accomplish this—even though for a time Sei thought potion-making was her real job.

Now that the setting is out in the countryside, the cast from the institute won't appear as often, so I apologize to Johan and Jude fans. I do plan to have everyone return to the palace eventually, so I hope you enjoy reading about Sei's easygoing(?) life for the time being.

The only guy from the palace who came with Sei was Knight Commander Albert. *The Saint's Magic Power is Omnipotent* is supposed to be a romance series, but there isn't much romance in this book, so I'm sure his feelings are hurt. I feel bad for him. Sei has a low level in romance, so their relationship isn't really progressing, but since he's with her right now, I'd like their relationship to progress a *little* bit. However, Sei being who she is, it'll probably be at a turtle's pace. That's part of living an easygoing life, so I hope you'll warmly watch over their relationship.

While I'm hoping to develop her relationship with Albert, we met a bunch of new characters this volume. Each of them fills a certain type of niche, and Leo fills the one that's all about muscles. I bet you're wondering why I created him. It just so happened that when I was coming up with the plot for this volume, weight training was all the rage. I came up with the idea of having a character that was more muscular than the people found in the palace, and thus Leo was born. It had nothing to do with the fact that many people, including Editor W and M-sensei, who is kind to me every day, love muscles. And it had *absolutely* nothing to do with the fact that I like bulging biceps and deltoids and wanted to see Shuri-sensei's muscular illustrations.

Speaking of Leo and his marvelous muscles, he's the opposite of his outward appearance in that he's not a muscle head. Grand Magus Yuri Drewes already fills that role, so Leo might just wind up becoming the comedic foil. At least, that's what I thought while writing the ending to Volume Three. While he's not a muscle head, Leo's still a bit rough around the edges, so I think he just might get a bit closer to Sei, and Albert just might get more distraught as a result. Huh? Wait, wasn't I trying to get Sei and Albert closer together? That's odd. Yeah. Well, characters don't always act as you'd assume... Sorry, Albert!

Yasuyuki Shuri-sensei did the illustrations for this volume as well. Thank you so much for your wonderful illustrations. In particular, I love Leo's upper arms on the cover. Truly a feast for the eyes. Err, I mean, thank you! You come up with such handsome character designs, and I feel all my fatigue from work fade away every time I look at the cover and opening illustration pages. T-sensei said that hot guys in your story are good for your health, and I think she might be right. This makes me grateful to Shuri-sensei all over again for coming up with such lovely character designs.

Not only is this series being published as a physical book, but it's being turned into a manga series as well. And on top of that, they even made a commercial for it to air on TV. As someone who can't draw, I was over the moon just to see my characters be illustrated, but this year I'll even be able to hear their voices. That's right—they actually made an audio drama for *The Saint's Magic Power is Omnipotent*! When I heard about this, I couldn't believe it, and I just couldn't stop smiling.

The drama's setting is a date with the Knight Commander Albert Hawke of the Knights of the Third Order. I still haven't listened to it as of writing this, but I know who they cast. One of the cast members sounds really hot. Genuinely hot. I hope all of Albert's fans give it a listen. The drama will be made available online, so please check out Kadokawa's home page.

Finally, thank you for reading up until this point. I made you wait for Volume Three's release, but I'm going to do my best to get Volume Four out as soon as possible. I hope we'll meet again soon!